CW00553473

WORDLESS THREADS

ELIZABETH WILDE McCORMICK

Brigand
London

Brigand Press,
All contact: info@brigand.london

British Library Cataloguing-in-Publication Data

A catalogue record for this book is
available from the British Library
Printed and Bound in Great Britain by
Datum Creative Media Ltd
www.datum.agency

ISBN: 978-1-912978-37-3

*For Maureen Wilde 'Mo'; and for
Simon, Kate and Nicky Wilde*

Also by
Elizabeth Wilde McCormick

Non Fiction
The Heart Attack Recovery Book 1984, 1989 Optima

Surviving Breakdown 1988, 1990, 1997 Vermillion

Healing The Heart 1994 Optima

Living On The Edge 1997,2007 Sage

Change For The Better, personal development
through practical psychotherapy
1990, 2002, 2008, 2012, 2017. Sage

With Dr Leisa Freeman:
Your Heart and You 2002 Piatkus

With Nigel Wellings:
Transpersonal Psychotherapy, theory and practice 200 Sage

Nothing To Lose, Psychotherapy, Buddhism and Living Life.
2004, 2012 Woodyard Publications

Present With Suffering 2022 Confer/Karnac Books

Fiction
The Pale Green Room. Brigand 2018

The Ruthless Furnace. Brigand 2019

Acknowledgements

I first became interested in what are called cryptic pregnancies in 1989. My sister-in-law Maureen Wilde said, 'you're never going to let this go are you, Liz?' Sadly, she died in 2013 and I miss her very much but throughout writing this novel her presence has been there.

Dear Mo, thank you.

I did quite a bit of research into the subject with the help of Carrie McCormick, an experienced natural midwife in the USA. Research was also carried out by my granddaughter Isabelle Wilde. A huge thank you to you both for your hard work and for our conversations.

My colleague and writing buddy Steve Potter and I met each month to discuss the progress of our writing. Over the last three years he has seen the development of Wordless Threads and been extremely helpful with feedback, encouraging me to strengthen Dr Max's character and resolve. I thank you dear Steve for all our conversations.

As ever I am truly grateful to my close friends who have encouraged me to complete this third and final part of the Dr Max trilogy.

I thank Annalee Curran, Margaret Landale, Gill Wilson, Ann Shearer, for their friendship and support. Linda Hartley read the passages connected to conception and I drew inspiration from her work on embodiment, on embryology and from her book *The Fluid Nature of Being* published by Handspring.

Dr Wasyl Nimenko sent me detailed reports from his work with soldiers on Salisbury Plain and he also read through the chapters involving the Plain. I extend many thanks for his support and friendship.

Editor Elaine Leek, who has edited several of my titles, read through the initial draft and helped me with continuity and timelines.

I thank Peter Holland for his support and Brigand for publication of the book.

Chapter 1

'How could I not know she was living inside me?'

Even after all these years the sentence still arises of its own accord, and I let it linger, allowing time to ponder on the nature of the spaces in which the words come into view. My younger self might well have judged the words a tease. But they are a signal for me to stand back from thoughts and give opportunity for something that has been hidden to arise, something that can only appear in silence. I have become accustomed to saying 'Ah, there you are.' It's as if some life form, unshared in consciousness but already present inside me, is now able to appear. I welcome it.

Agnes. Those early months where she presented like a whipped puppy, crouched over, with no memory of the new life that once grew inside her. From time to time, I see those eyes again, deep set, blue, intense, carrying the light of a native intelligence hidden beneath the hurt of a wounded animal.

It's seven years now since she first came to me and two years since we completed our work together. Seven years! I think of her now as she recently asked to come and see me again. Her request has sent me into deep reflections on our years together.

Agnes, how we lit a beacon of light together from out of the shared deepest darkness! Darkness I had sensed but not known was also inside me. It was her story that brought her to me; of her daughter, destined not to be known whilst inside her or to live outside her; but now a presence for ever. And an ancestral past equally tragic. How these layers of life took form as we sat, side by side, watching each season as it bowed to us across the garden. She brought light from the very essence of her extraordinary being, as well as her dark story.

At our first meeting I asked her where she would like to begin. She had shrugged and looked down. There was then a long silence, which started to become uncomfortable, so I had asked gently, 'Can you tell me what has happened to you over these last two years in your own words, something of what you remember, no matter how small.'

She had looked shocked. 'But you know don't you, you

know what I've done ...'

I paused before saying something probably rather formal like: 'This is an exploratory first meeting, Agnes. I really want to hear your own words and memories. Therapy is a collaborative process, we are in it together, going with the unknown.'

She sat so still, thin under her oversized clothes, her rather beautiful delicate hands clenched together. She often turned her head from side to side as if trying to shake something away. I wondered what she saw when she closed her eyes or what might haunt her with open eyes. Eyes so blue, so clear. Her gaze seemed to touch something in my chest near to the heart. I realised at that first meeting that there was a connection between us, mysterious, and unusual for me.

I wondered then, where would this young woman take me? Where might we travel together, or let each other go? As I had these thoughts, I heard my dear friend Philip's voice: 'Be brave, be bold. Step into the unknown in both of you.'

Now I do know! What an adventure. I remember that first session clearly. I was my usual calm and controlling self, trying to keep peace. Peace over what was to be utterly turbulent!

She was silent for what seemed a long time and I found myself speaking again, probably sounding rather pompous. 'Your understanding of everything that has happened is really important, Agnes, and we have plenty of time, there is no rush.' I remember speaking slowly, feeling my way with the words that arose, wanting to engage her. 'This process offers the opportunity for deep listening, and hearing, for both of us.'

She had shrugged. 'I know, I know all that. Carole's told me. I'm here because of her.' Big sigh. 'But it doesn't help what I've done.'

'It's good that you're here, Agnes. You've made a start by coming, it's brave. And at any time, you have the freedom to leave.' I worried that I was being too serious and that she might not understand. 'Through this we both find out new things, things we couldn't have known before.' I tried to make it all sound reasonable, but something was not quite right and that feeling in my chest persisted. She was watching me intently.

'Hopefully this shared process will help you to find moments when you can meet this very painful experience with some understanding.'

Her gaze went immediately to her lap, to the thin hands with her scarf wrapped around them. 'I don't think that will ever be possible.'

There followed a painful pause. Her voice was nearly a whisper and I had to lean a little forward to hear her.

'She comes to me in my dreams. Sometimes she speaks: "How could you not know I was there. I wanted to land. To land with you. How could you not see me?"'

Chapter 2

It was Carl who introduced me to Agnes. When I play the second of Chopin's Nocturnes now, the feelings that arise remind me of the many shifts in awareness both Carl and Agnes awakened all those years ago.

I had worked with Carl after his return from serving in the army in Afghanistan. He was badly injured and came to the clinic I had set up struggling with PTSD and identity. He had intense and furious feelings about the army being the 'only option' for him after leaving school at 16. He was aware of the paradox – he had joined feeling hopeful he would find something of shared community there, do some good for his country, and have perhaps something resembling a decent family life. But the army disciplines and invitations to aggression felt like an unhappy continuation of his earlier life. He had also felt very isolated. He struggled with feelings of being what he called an imposter, an 'imposter man'. He had inherited a strong man's body but not the will or gore to act in the way he had been told made a 'proper man'. He would beat his chest and say: 'I don't know who's in there.' During his early life he had been passed around different family members after his single mother died of an overdose; he grew up feeling wretched and homeless but having to please and succumb to others in order to belong, and, as we understood during out work together, feel safe. There were regular beatings from different family members. He coped by shutting down all feeling, by hiding in any available space. Hiding was a powerful theme. He had learned to hide his fear of being seen as effeminate and the ridicule he had sustained from others over his natural gentleness, his interest in colours and shapes, in soft fabrics. He learned to hide his love of music for fear of it being taken away from him out of spite.

Music sustained him, especially when he could hold tunes and cadences in his head and heart whilst on patrol. It was the quiet presence of someone living in one of the streets he walked down to school, some distance from his own home, that had awakened him to the possibility of life offering a different quality and attitude, opposite from his home life. This woman was a pianist and Carl would leave home early so that he could stop near her open window close enough to hear the wondrous sounds, magic to him, callings from another world. Unknown to him she had noticed his presence near her window, and eventually leaned out of the window to speak. She then invited him in to listen as she played. He still held the notes of the Chopin Nocturne with great joy and gratitude. She must have been touched by the open amazement on his face for she offered to teach him the piano for free, something he kept hidden from any family member. He pretended to be at football practice. Her spontaneous kindness, seeing something no one else had seen in him, laid down one of the most important foundations for his life.

One day he had arrived early for his appointment with me; my garden door was open, and he heard me playing Chopin. He came into the room with tears in his eyes. 'Doc,' he said, 'we have music in our souls!' I stood up and he took my place at the piano, which by then I had in the consulting room, and he played that second Nocturne, turning round to look at me smiling before he returned to the keys and rushed through Chopin's 'Minute Waltz' with great enthusiasm. When he finished, his brown eyes were blazing. 'Those two pieces, – opposites: that first one could sound out for what I discovered in secret and have silently in my soul and then that last! A real show-off piece. But, he gave a huge sigh: 'that's how I've been living isn't it? At least on the surface! Too fast, no pause, hurrying, never stop to think, to reflect, too much … on and on … never to feel what's in there, like music makes us,' pressing his hand to his chest as he spoke. 'No pause, just always breathless.'

He was right and I marvelled at how perceptive he was; he played well, and I wondered how he had continued to nourish this talent when he was in the army. The sharing of music and its potential for transforming feeling and attitude became an important bond between us. It led us to search for sound, tune, scale, and note, for different emotions when there were no words for feelings, no words for body longings and expressions. At first, he would look puzzled when I asked him what he was feeling and he would move toward the piano to find a note that most suited, sound it out with his voice and then eventually settle on a place in his body which seemed to match feeling. He could then stay with this feeling as the beginning of communication, we could spend time with this and return to it easily when appropriate. Music had always, since teenage years, offered him an unnamed and different dimension of feeling to which he could submit without being overwhelmed. I was to learn that this was a strong link he had with Agnes, for she too had discovered the power of music during her early life. But for both, it had to remain hidden for fear it might be destroyed or taken away from them. Agnes said once, with such sadness: 'She might have destroyed my hands.' I was shocked deeply and silenced by this – her hands destroyed by her own mother.

Carl reminded me of another soldier I had seen, Frank Bright, whose background was similar and many of his fine qualities had been negated or smothered and never realised. He had to commit a crime and bear the terrible consequences in order to find his way to a decent equilibrium, for his unnamed feelings to be recognised and named. I remembered how Frank loved to sing and that it was singing that allowed him to enter a world of friendliness and sharing. It was the overture to the healing of his many emotional wounds.

Carl asked to see me a few years after our work was completed. As he entered my room he brought in a vision of transformation. The sun lit his long hair, carefully groomed, his smooth face was beautifully made up, including what had always been the extravagant eyelashes over those deep brown eyes; and he wore elegant female clothes. 'I thought I'd give you a surprise, Doc,' he said, smiling.

'So, you went for it then, Carl. Good for you!'

'This is me! I've found my true home. I went for it. I'm Carole now, and I feel great!'

He was clearly happy. During our work we had discussed the possibility of his taking this final physical step, but he had been uncertain.

He read my face and said, 'You're not surprised are you, Doc? You didn't think I'd end up going the whole way, doing this?' He gave a little twirl of his full purple skirt sending his beads and earrings into a frenzy, and smiled, mischievously.

I invited him to sit down, thinking more before I said anything. I was aware of wanting to be careful around him –

now her – watching my language and my possible assumptions, what is now termed unconscious bias. I had known the person before me as Carl, male, and now I was to know Carole as both male Carl and female Carole. Them.

'How do you like to be addressed?' I asked.

'I'm just Carole, Doc. I'm not bothered by he, she, them or trans. I've not joined the trans community. For me it's just private. I'm glad you will be someone who will know me in both bodies.' He tapped his chest. 'I'm me and allowed to be me.'

I was suddenly interested to know more, much more. The person in front of me was a person I had known well within the structure of a therapy. A person with a body that had received so much hatred, aggression and violence, had harboured often impossible fear and rage, and which, when he had learned to listen safely and kindly, had led the way to transformation. Since our meeting I've had many, many more thoughts about the potential for communication and language available by living as consciously as possible in a human body; and how many of us find this difficult. Finding words for feelings often hidden deep inside a human body takes time, trust and love. But the release of both body and feeling is often the fount of creativity and certainly relief. What they can reveal, given enough safe space to be listened to and tolerated, can bring about real transformation.

Carole then sat down and looked suddenly serious. 'I've wanted to come and see you for a while. I want to thank you for the way you helped me to see for myself what I really needed. You gave me time to listen to myself. I had no idea this was what I was looking for all along.' She gestured to her now clearly female body.

'Thank you,' I said, smiling, surprised by a surge in my chest.

'Without our work I might have rushed into the physical changes destructively. As a defence, in rage, I think. To protest and give two fingers to those who called me names.' She shrugged and looked sad. 'Or done nothing, continued in destructive depression.' She looked up, her face full of softness and what I took to be gratitude. 'In the clinic I found I had quite a different form of courage than that required o the battlefield.' With these words we sat in silence together.

Since seeing Carl, now Carole, and seeing Agnes, I've also thought much more about the hidden power of real in-depth conversation between two people, verbal and non-verbal, and within a trusted safe therapeutic container. It's a precious vessel indeed. The wordless threads within relational conversation weave a new tapestry. Time to ponder in all the invited spaces, shared and in between meetings. Therapists never know where patients might take them or what might emerge in this relational communication, particularly in the spaces between words. And I ponder also, often, on the movement invited by music. The body that leads the way, in subtle movements, in gestures, in blinking, gasps, clutching, each one language without words. And that words can be found if they are needed. Both Carl and Agnes showed me this. Sound itself, created to be shared, can sound a note deep inside us, opening the way to our individual needs, opening us to something yet to be realised. I wondered if music could sound a note to something deep inside us that is mainly gender-free. Carole was working in a help centre for people struggling with gender identity. Agnes had stumbled into their premises thinking it was another kind of clinic where she might find help. Carole was there when she arrived and began supporting her to find what she needed. Over time, she felt Agnes should see someone professionally. Agnes story had also led her into researching into what are called cryptic pregnancies.

As Carole stood to leave, I said, 'It's been good to see you, Carole.' I really meant it. I then said, slowly, 'I'm curious. Agnes' loss is tragic, but I'm wondering why you thought of encouraging her to come here, to me.' She was silent, and I started to feel awkward. 'I mean, what is it that made you think Agnes and I might be suited to work together?'

Carole remained thoughtful, serious.

'There is unlived life in all of us, Doc, waiting to be born if it possibly can. Born,' she raised her arm, 'born to live, live. Not raised in hope then die of ignorance.' She had looked at me intensely before putting her hand lightly on my chest saying, 'I think you will know when you meet her.'

I was indeed drawn to Agnes as soon as we met, and I too began reading about what had plunged her into another world. Cryptic pregnancy. The phrase felt odd, misleading. All the cases reported were intriguing, all very different. What stirred my interest was that each one had their own story to tell. The 'event' of carrying a child without knowing seemed to call on many different factors. It could not be reduced to a psychological label such as denial, psychosis, or avoidance. My task was to understand Agnes' story, allow her the spaciousness to take her time; and to see if she was able to bring to life – I was aware of the pun - how she became pregnant, what had happened during those following months, and develop her own curiosity about the entire process and why it went unnoticed, especially by her. And to find a way to mourn what might have been.

I had also started reading about embryology so that I might understand more. As I read and tried to formulate some plan of how to invite her into this exploration, I realised that broaching this very personal, and painful, subject with Agnes would have to wait until we had established real trust. Indeed, it might well prove impossible. I remember sitting, pondering on these encounters as I listened to Rachmaninov – Piano Concerto No. 2. Such underground power there. The echo of a heartbeat. The questioning, and hope, in the rise and fall of the piano, the deep calls from the orchestra's bass. A work of great feeling, and contradiction. I thought about the difficulty for a man imagining what it might be like to carry a child inside and was aware this might be an issue working with Agnes. It's not something I've ever considered or been interested in, but I know other men who are truly fascinated, who express a real desire to know what it might be like, imaging the movements of a child living within them. Some who have openly wished they could have carried a child inside. In my reading I came across many new ideas and associations of my own; it was a revelation. Those times were to become transformative for me.

And now, as I watch the stillness of my garden and allow Rachmaninov to resound within me again, I am reminded about the link between the heart and loss, often felt physically in the chest area as an aching heaviness. Some losses can be named and receive support and help until each of us is able to recognise and nurture our own suffering ourselves. The impact of some forms of loss are created silently when we have to hold feeling within, when we have no voice. They are so impossible they remain inside us. Times when it is only denial and repression of our vulnerability that helps us survive fear. Fear of judgement, fear of getting close to another, of opening one's heart and to let in love, to receive it and treasure it. For opening one's heart means being vulnerable. It made me think about Philip, my closest friend who died some years ago. His extravert style and ability to amuse with stories concealed a deep loneliness. I can see him now on our last walk together, speaking about the paths of life we enter. He had stopped and become wistful, spreading out his large strong hands. 'When we decide to choose fully what has already chosen us, something we've never considered but already there can arise.' He turned to me and pressed my chest. A precursor to Carole's touch. I was to find out how true this was.

What we owe to ancestors and friends that lead the way! How we must learn to receive, especially love, and how extraordinarily difficult it can be to simply recognise that love is there, intended for us.

I get up now, full of the heartbeat of memory and walk around my small garden in South London where mimosa flowers in late winter, bringing its generous exotic fragrance into what often appears barren, just before spring announces herself fully. It reminds me again of the first spring all those years ago after I had agreed to work with Agnes. I can see her walking down my street with what I came to call her 'heron walk', headfirst, head and eyes moving from left to right, on alert, ready to fly at any moment. To fly away from terror, always lurking, ready to grab her.

It was three months into our work when she said those words again: 'How could I not know she was living inside me.' It was certainly the most lucid sentence she had spoken in our weekly meetings. I was relieved then by the seeming awareness behind her words, as if she was coming to sense that there could have been a part of her that 'knew' but which had been shut down. I remember now how quickly my own thoughts had arisen, of my sister, Margaret. Did some part of me 'know' that another living being, Margaret, was living and growing beside me when we were in our own mother's womb? The first thought was quickly followed by: should I have known? But then, even our mother didn't know she was expecting twins.

I remember trying hard to focus then as Agnes was looking at me with those huge blue eyes, a child's eyes, wide-eyed in shock still.

I was probably awkward, saying, 'That's a difficult, painful realisation, Agnes, but it's a truth. A truth about your experience. From what you have told me, you did not know.'

She looked down, tears always near now, falling easily. 'It's so wrong isn't it, Doctor. How could I be so unaware, so out of touch. There's so much wrong with me.'

Chapter 3

Before human conception there is a dance in a female body between ovum and sperm. A human being comes into existence when these two cells meet in the fallopian tubes and join before moving down into the uterus, and the next dance begins, one of expanding and condensing forms animated by the breath of life. All hidden from view, from conscious awareness. It's a wonder.

I'm reading this listening to Vivaldi's Four Seasons. Autumn. It is melodic, purposeful and haunting, I imagined it might illustrate the quivering temptation between sperm and ovum, each dancing together in very different ways. I was surprised by noticing my body reacting as I read and listened, swaying slightly. It's as if it understood something of this dance without my having to think about it. I read about the speedy competitiveness of the sperm which, in its multiplicity must compete with millions of others to get into the ovum, the main goal. Each sperm has an elongated shape with a long tail, styled for penetration, whilst the ovum is spherical. It made me smile then as I do now when I think of the many stereotypes that can be created between men and women from this one biological fact. Different male forms of penetration that emerge as focus, single mindedness, aggression and competitiveness; female receptivity, receiving the igniting force of the male – how this can become close to qualities of passivity, submission; and there are certainly ways in which the passivity and fragility can become fused, even a form of control.

Emily! and the hold her fragility had over me in our marriage. But at the time I could not see it objectively, I just felt responsible for her and her moods and keen to help her. But my own passivity to responding appropriately, especially when she was unreasonably demanding only perpetuated her neediness despite our somewhat feeble attempts to live more equally together. I also think back again now to those days when I was learning afresh about this male–female biology and imagining these dances between sperm and ovum. I found them fascinating. Again, there is that question. Does it all start in utero? Is it all biological, hormonal, predetermined by genes? Does it matter? Again, words limit these experiences.

But just reading these chapters, lent to me by Carole, awakened my curiosity and initiated an exploration within myself. I pondered more, not for the first time, about my own capacity for appropriate male aggression and competitiveness. For penetration of any kind. I was saddened by my lack of what is seen as these biological inheritances. Had I ever had any? If so, where had they been for most of my life? Had I suppressed my maleness or never been able to recognise it? Was I unable to feel it in my body, as Agnes had never felt her child moving in hers?

Philip used to chide me for never getting angry or fiery and thrusting forward with it: 'You're not even mildly cross, man, when you should be.' He danced around me, waving his pelvis and with his hands raised in a potential boxer's punch. 'C'mon, let's have a good fight.' And I always laughed nervously, probably even did a little nervous dance around him. Even though my missing capacity for anger and aggression was often encountered and commented on throughout all the therapy and analysis I received, I still tended not to get cross properly, as I noticed others can. Now I know only too well that I can be good at self-deception, at cheating even, and I watch out for it. As Carole said when she was in Carl's body, 'Who's in there? Who's real in there?' Sweeping his hand down his torso before beating his chest and howling.

I know now that I am not a fake man. Even in my mid-sixties, I've had a wonderful teacher. How lucky I am now. But then, working with Agnes and her impossible lost life taught me so much. A real in-depth curiosity began to be awakened as well as so many of my senses! It was a wonder. Elongated with a long tail. All my years of celibacy after Oxford, choosing a celibate marriage. – what had my tail been doing? As I mused on all this, I could see Philip smiling and nodding as he sits, playing music – probably something by Sting. Then I hear his voice, on one of our walks after he had tempted me to a date with a particular woman, he had his own eye on: 'Got to get a grip, man, give it a go. You can't avoid women all your life. Take some risks for God's sake. Get it up.' He did a playful dance as we walked with his dog, Belle, across the heath. He had had many women since I'd known him but only risked short term intimacy. 'You've gone too much a softie since that business in Oxford.' We had walked in silence for a while. He then stopped and took me by the shoulders looking serious and quoted Yeats again: 'Release that unknown rough beast that slouches to be born.'

What might have helped me listen then? But timing is everything, like opportunity. Then it was as if I could only analyse, take control through thinking. And what of Yeats rough beast in me? I was too much in control to let a rough beast take any course. I think again of Carole when she was Carl and his words: 'I'm a pretend man, Doc. I don't really know who it is who lives in there,' pressing his chest. But he found out. He let his rough beast find her way to be born.

As I mused on this and as Vivaldi's music intensified with a change of key I was transported back in time to my undergraduate years in Oxford, to my secret affair with Frances, my tutor's wife. I closed my eyes then and allowed my body to take me there. It remembered the way only too well. How we made love for hours, how she teased me, tempted me repeatedly. I fell for it every time, I could not get enough. I had never known such complete body emotion and mind captivation, that pure intoxication merging on madness Shakespeare knew only too well. That red hair with its mass of impossible curls, the smell of her, those eyes, utterly compelling. What she taught me about sex, all kinds of sex, about lust, longing, compulsion, and, eventually, about guilt. During all those hours of love-making – was it love? – her husband, my tutor, was giving lectures just a few streets away. Those days of delicious dancing bodies, always hungry for more. Those heady nights when he was away, and we had a whole eight hours together coupled with the tenson of what would happen if he arrived back unexpectedly.

To be inside all that softness with my hardness. A hardness that seemed to have its own force and was like nothing I had ever experienced. I was most certainly the penetrating male partner then, my body coming truly alive, and she encouraged me, she showed me all the ways to pleasure. She took me from shy, celibate, inhibited adolescence into sexual manhood. She was lover, initiator, conspirator. The scent of her perfume – I've never come across it again.

Then there was the child. The child who might have

been. Seeing Agnes brought the energy and memory of that time and the child into the present moment. I still shiver now when I remember. The child I might have had would now be over forty and I might have even been a grandparent. I can feel shocked all over again. By the obvious deep loss of it that I had blanked out for so long.

The child Agnes might have had would be walking around now, learning, loving, enjoying, and Agnes a parent. If denial was the core state for Agnes, I was in it too. There's more than just this, I know; maybe it was all more than this. Creating life without intention is shocking, frightening. It's a brave person, or perhaps simply a passive one, who goes along with it. Bringing a life into the world is a responsibility, always. I realised, with a heavy heart, that responsibility was always my default position, a learned trap, that and keeping the peace at all costs. I'd never felt free. Nor had Agnes.

Frances aborted our child without discussion; the unwanted, unknown to me, child. When did she know she was pregnant? Did she know when we were still seeing each other, and I was entering her body with such excitement of my own I had little thought for hers except what a wonderful receptive vehicle it was. She had said she had contraception 'all sorted' and I never gave it another thought. Why did she not tell me? My heart can still fill when I reflect back. Frances always set the times of our meetings of course and had been avoiding me for weeks so I knew something was up. When I finally managed to see her again – I just turned up at their flat one morning when I knew her husband was delivering a lecture, I could see how distraught she was. She, reluctantly, let me in saying that I could not stay long.

I asked her repeatedly what was wrong and eventually she told me. My shock was physical, like a bolt of lightning through my gut. I was speechless. When I said: 'but why, why did you not tell me?' she snorted and said, 'And what would you have done, scholarship boy?' Tears welled up in my eyes and she softened and said, 'You'd probably have offered to marry me wouldn't you, soft duck. Can you imagine that? My husband, your tutor, in high regard of you and your fine intellect and scholarship, cuckolded, scorned by an upstart. He might have slain you.'

I was shocked all over again. Silenced. This kind of naked female power and aggression was too catastrophic for my innocent 20-year-old self. I'd not come across this in her. She was, for me, my glorious initiator of lust and pleasure, the total physical absorption that bypassed thought as I just let my body follow hers. Certainly, leading the way. After this I never did again. I sealed something firmly shut.

Then she said quietly, 'He would never have known about the child if the termination hadn't gone wrong.' She looked at me sadly, 'I could have died you see.' I was shocked again. And responsible. I had created this.

'I haemorrhaged badly and collapsed. Marcus was called by the hospital and that's how he found out. He knows it couldn't have been his child, he's infertile. Mumps. So, it would have been even worse I think.' She had looked sad, older suddenly, as she wrapped her shawl around herself more tightly as if wanting her fierceness back.

'And if I'd gone on with it, after that what? You, me and a child huddled in some bedsit, your whole career ruined by lust.' Her eyes closed. I went toward her, but she pushed me away. 'No. I did the right thing.'

'But, but, didn't you want a child?'

'Yes, I did. But not like this.'

There was a dense silence between us, dark and dense.

'What we had was fun,' she said quietly. 'Just fun. You would have tired of me soon enough. When you met a young woman your own age.'

I was shocked, gutted some people might have said, stuck for words. I remember pacing up and down the floor of their sitting room, with its shelves of wonderful books. 'But, but …' I stammered, trying to gain some control, 'that's your interpretation. You never thought to consider me in it all.' She just sat, dry-eyed, looking down. I remember saying, 'You've had all the power. Power over life and death.' I'm glad at least I managed to say that.

She pouted. I'd never seen her do that and it reminded me of my mother when she wanted her own way. Chilling.

'It's my body,' Frances eventually responded, looking at me

quite fiercely. 'What we had was just lust, fun, but just lust.' She then stood up. 'Go' she said her mouth fixed. 'Go and grow up.'

That's all it was to her. Lust with consequences that had to be paid for. For me it was so, so much more. I think of all this now. My initiation into the glorious wonders of the body, my own and hers. Male female. How sex can be when you let go completely, how it can become addictive. I'd not feasted enough and wanted more. This was my still adolescent self. My part in it all had led to death.

I stood still, the grey colour of the sitting room walls closing in on my crushed self. After a while I left, shattered. It marked the end of our relationship and the end of Frances' marriage.

That time in Oxford, my last year as an undergraduate. What magic Frances wove, what she showed me that was not to last, that remained as mere potential, but born only to be buried; the first woman I ever slept with – and, until just over two years ago, the last. I had been totally, completely under her spell. My reading about conception had begun to awaken me to the past and my involvement. Vivaldi long completed I sat in silence with the body memory of that day. I then heard the lyrics of a song sung by Sting that I had played over and over in my head in the following years. For me his music would always recall physical passion.

'In his arms she fell as her hair came down … When we walked in fields of gold.'

'Her hair came down ...'

I got lost for hours in that hair. What would I have done if she had told me she was pregnant? I was 20, about to take finals, her husband was my tutor. Would I have given it all up to become a father and husband?

I never saw Frances again after that day. She moved away and I had to endure the distraught face of my tutor. She had kept her promise and he did not know I was the guilty man. I then buried the memory, achieved a PhD in Cambridge and went to Switzerland to join a monastery. Apart from some confessional times there I had banned the whole event from my thoughts. I took on and married Emily, sad, damaged Emily, now living with her lover Shirley. Was a celibate marriage my penance for my sin with Frances and her child? Did I have to offer penance for my sin by trying to rescue needy others? Did I make an unconscious vow to suffer silently like a martyr? And to remain celibate for another forty years. Had I paid enough?

Working with Agnes brought these memories to life again. My time during those heady Oxford days, full of images, smells, sensations. I also had to think more about the nature of burying thought and event particularly after an event which could be judged forbidden, sinful, harmful. And to think about poisoning. Think about how it's not just substances that poison. What sadness's, and what gifts, can arise from these times – but later, much later. If Agnes had been conscious of a life growing inside her, what might she have done? I knew clearly after the first few months of sitting with her that she was telling the truth when she said she had no idea at any time that she might be pregnant. We sat for some time with this paradox. Her body was extremely thin, it was hard to imagine her pregnant without it being noticed externally.

There is a memory now of sitting with my first analyst when I was training. So many silences! I was comfortable enough as I was used to them, but there were times when I drifted off, practising in my mind and hands a difficult piece of Rachmaninov that I was attempting to learn. But one day in spring, as I sat looking out into his garden, some of what must have been stored as bitterness emerged, which startled me. Perhaps my first glimpse of anger. He let me speak, on and on I went, allowing something of a deep-seated unfairness I was feeling to enter the room. Anger even, at what I might have had, love I might have had, parents, sister, lover, child all gone before I had a chance to feel loved fully, to receive it fully, and to give love freely. Even then I felt guilty for speaking angrily about my fate.

'You are allowed to be angry, Max', he had said.

I had probably shrugged. I remember feeling sadder than ever, and hopeless. We would speak of course about my early life. I used to wonder what I might have done differently to win my parents' interest and I mentioned this even though embarrassed. I had said, probably in a sad little boy voice: 'I just longed for any form of real contact with them, anything.' I remember there was some bitterness in me as I said, 'All I got was crumbs.'

He had allowed a decent pause, familiar now, to allow each of us to feel the depth of the emotional need, for it to have a proper place of recognition and respect. Then he said, 'There's nothing wrong with crumbs.'

I was startled then. It was a surprise. I didn't believe him, I felt as if I was being fobbed off, as if all I was worthy of was crumbs. But since then, I've learned to gather and respect crumbs, for myself and for my patients, and to let the crumbs have a life and reveal themselves. To let them have a dance. To even form bread and cakes.

Having heard Sting through thinking about Philip earlier, I hear him again now: 'something in our minds will always stay … lest we forget how fragile we are'.

Chapter 4

Two years before we met, Agnes was found on Salisbury Plain in the autumn rain after her friend Anna had reported her missing. She had no memory of how she arrived there from London, where she was living. Some walkers found her lying within sight of Stonehenge, curled up in a foetal position, weeping silently. Her body and clothes were covered in a sandy wetness and bloodstained. Her arms were wound tightly round her chest. The walkers called an ambulance and waited with her. She screamed and fought when the ambulance crew tried to move her onto the trolley. After being taken to a local hospital, she had to be sedated due to her screams and rigidity. Eventually she was undressed by the nursing staff.

The dead body of her new-born daughter was strapped around her chest. She never saw her child again after the hospital staff separated them. She was assessed by the psychiatric team and eventually referred to the Maudsley Hospital in London, where she began an attempt at recovery from this huge ordeal with help from social workers and psychologists.

These details emerged slowly, in no specific order as Agnes and I began our work. I learned also that it was after her close friend Anna had a child that Agnes began to regress and went wandering. She had stumbled into the clinic where Carole was working hoping she might find something, 'a helping hand' was how she described it, her head bowed. Carole had listened, kindly, and offered to help. Agnes had no conscious memory of being found by the walkers or being admitted to the local hospital. But she knew that she had 'done something dreadful' and been taken to a 'psychiatric' hospital. Carole managed to find the name of the first hospital and spent some time checking it out with Agnes. She found the name of a senior staff member who had worked in maternity at the time Agnes was admitted and wrote to her asking if Agnes might also write and ask for more information about her time there. When she received no reply, she telephoned different departments and eventually found the appropriate channel for what she felt Agnes really needed. She appealed to the hospital staff she was able to contact saying that now, two years on, Agnes wanted to get help to find out what had happed. By using friendliness and charm, and her increasing knowledge of complex cases, Carole had been able to discover the name of the couple who found Agnes on Salisbury Plain and encouraged Agnes to write to thank them. But when we first met, Agnes had not yet felt able to do this. She had looked at me earnestly as she said she had 'wanted to do the right thing.' But she also said that her courage failed her. She could not bear any of it. It was 'too, too awful'.

Carole also told me that the hospital staff had arranged for a post-mortem of her child and that her daughter was stillborn, she had died in utero. If she had been born alive Agnes might have had to face charges of infanticide. The hospital also told Carole that the scattering of the ashes of the child's body had been according to their traditions at that time. But Agnes had no memory of being offered to be part of this and had never been to visit the site where the ashes were scattered.

Her sense of emptiness was evident, and she felt lost, also puzzled and at times really confused. Had it not been for her chancing into the clinic where Carole was working, the whole experience might have lain buried, like her dead child. She might have ended her own life. When we met it felt as if she was living a half-life, deeply depressed, full of shame and sorrow.

Walking alongside listening and sympathetic others, speaking of what she could recollect of these last years, was both agonising and revelatory, but an important journey for her. It was a journey with no goal other than recollections and allowing what had been repressed to find consciousness safely. I couldn't know whether she would ever reach understanding. But we travelled together with hope for what venturing into the unknown might bring. I thought often of the poetry of T. S. Eliot's Wasteland where the faith, the hope and the love are all in the waiting. The active waiting of shared communication.

To begin with Agnes and I met several times in an exploratory way to see if we might work usefully together. Even though she had no awareness of being pregnant and giving birth she knew that it had happened because of the dramatic events surrounding her hospital admission. And because there was written evidence – it had all been recorded. I was new to this presentation and curious to research it. Also, working with Agnes invited me more deeply into the complex nature of awareness itself. My Buddhist meditation practice had helped to develop my understanding and experience of the open space offered by simple awareness, and to trust in it. The rising of thoughts, feelings and sensations could be simply noticed, named simply, but not followed. This showed me that the spaciousness that often resulted from remembering to stop and notice these moments gave me a certain freedom and helped me not to become so fixed in thoughts and ideas, even, at times closed down. It helped my work as a therapist not to jump into interpretation or analysis. Perhaps one of the fruits of the Oxford tragedy was my time in the monastery in Switzerland where I began to learn about what it meant be really present. Whilst I had always enjoyed the value of shared silence with patients, working with Agnes brought much more of this understanding and experience to the fore. It was when I simply stopped, put aside any psychological thoughts or interpretations and waited for what might emerge without hope or expectation that Agnes began to find her voice.

What I also learned acutely with Agnes was that the subtle arisings from within a traumatised body were at first unavailable to any form of consciousness, let alone understanding. It was simply too painful to pay attention. The need to be on automatic was an important form of survival for her. These tiny, microscopic communications needed time and safety for recognition, and only then, within the wordless spaces safely held and shared could words that matched sensation or feeling arise. Then what might be needed next could emerge. And very, very slowly; sometimes in a language not initially understood, but powerful in a way all of its own. Very similar to the therapeutic journey made with Carl but much more intense.

Agnes was then still, two years on from the birth, shocked, desperate, guilty and sad. Her account of that year before Salisbury Plain was hazy to begin with. Carole had helped to add in some of the details and encouraged Agnes to reveal more. What I knew was that, around the Christmas time before Salisbury Plain, she had had some sort of breakdown. From her early teens she had had to fight hard for her independence from her single mother, working as a waitress and cleaner to pay for music lessons and then getting into music school. She had left home as soon as possible and shared a flat with others whilst she built up her work as a piano and singing teacher in schools and also privately. But as she felt more and more unwell leading up to that Christmas time she'd had to cut down on her work, eventually having to give up the flat she rented for lack of funds. She had reluctantly returned to stay with her mother in the one-bedroomed flat where she grew up.

Living with her mother again was extremely painful and smacked of failure and defeat. In the early days of our work, she found it too difficult to speak of her mother and I knew that this was another area we had to inch our way carefully around. Her body flinched as she spoke of these times which had been clearly an extremely painful time for her. From what I was able to gather early on, she went out most days to keep practising on friends' pianos and occasionally did manage some teaching. Her voice was low, and her body slumped, the grey woven scarf was held tightly as she spoke of these times. I knew there was much more but that we must wait. When I asked her, tentatively, to tell me about her knowledge and interest in Salisbury Plain and why she had gone there she was silent for some time, looking down. When she looked up there were tears in her eyes. 'Salisbury Plain,' she said in a whisper. 'A place of magic. I visited when I was young, really young. I was taken out for the day. The woman was really kind. Kind.' She looked up, her tears flowing. 'I had never known such kindness. We found things there, special things, old things. It's a place of treasures, real treasures.' We sat together in silence with this sentence full of strong feeling. I knew we had shared something vital about the importance of kindness and treasure and would come back to it.

She stayed with her mother, except for the occasional times staying with friends for over a year. I imagined that it must have been deeply unpleasant for her. In the new year following the birth when she was still struggling and feeling unwell, her mother kept asking her 'what is wrong with you child.' Her mother would hit her regularly as she was growing up and she always feared for her hands. Her mother would get hold of them and squeeze.' You've only got time for piano keys haven't you.

No time for your own mother, after all I've done for you!'

I flinched as she said this. Then one day, tired of her mother's questioning Agnes blurted out that she had been pregnant the year before without knowing and given birth to a dead child on Salisbury Plain. 'That's why I was in hospital,' she said quietly having to face her mother's disbelief and fury.

'You disgust me,' her mother had said. 'Get out.' Her mother threw her out of the flat. Agnes spoke of this in a flat voice, on automatic.

I felt deeply shocked again by this cruelty. 'I am so, so sorry Agnes, that feels so harsh.'

Agnes spoke as if it was just how things were.

She had stayed with Anna for a while and by the time she and I met the following year she was living in a flat rented from a friend of Anna's husband, Mark, and she had been able to get her piano out of storage and have it with her. As well as taking on some pupils she had returned to work at the charity shop where she was known, for it gave her confidence to step out into the world again. When she spoke of the work there, and of beginning to give piano lessons there was huge warmth in her and a light in her blue eyes. Clearly, she was someone who naturally wanted to give to others. Working as a piano teacher gave her some solace; but her wounds were obvious in the way she was living, suspended inside her traumatised body. What encouraged her to take further steps was Carole's enthusiasm for the potential transformation that can occur when time is shared, and safe, in a chosen long-term communication with another. Carole had also generously given Agnes illustrations from her own time in therapy and came with Agnes to some of the sessions.

I had mixed feelings about that and at times felt that Carole was either testing or teasing me through her attentiveness to Agnes, or by showing off in various ways. Whilst I knew that she was helpful in her encouragement, there would be many times in the encounters between the three of us that were unnerving. Often, I would think: 'what am I being shown here?'

One day Carole said, 'Being here in this room with Dr Max has made me brave.' As she spoke, she lifted Agnes's hand, looking at her with real tenderness. 'It's bravery that's unseen, unrecognised, and not to do with force.' She had laughed then, 'It's not what I was brought up with! Bravery that's all brawn and muscle, sneering and knives.' She stood and made fists and brought them close to me, laughing.

When she came to me as Carl, he had eventually been prepared to notice his own suffering and be present with it in moments so that there was more spaciousness around it, more language or notes to express it and he became less reactive. We spoke of suffering often, and the nature of suffering and what it is that suffers. He had given himself time to begin to first tolerate and then understand the communications of his body and find the language in words, song or poetry that fitted. Now he was Carole, living life joyfully and fully having been transformed from learning to listen deeply to the language offered by his body.

In the beginning Agnes had said. 'All right I'll give it six goes.' We all smiled. She stayed for five years.

I can still picture her during those early days. Each time she came wearing the same oversized clothes bought randomly from charity shops and wrapped around her thin body carelessly, as if she didn't really live in a body. She sat so still, as if not breathing, her slim, elegant hands, musician's hands, clasped on her lap. Occasionally she would bend forward, folding herself over. Always she wore the same scarf, pale grey, see-through, knotted with what looked like cobwebs.

At first, I spoke too seriously and felt immediately embarrassed by my clumsiness. But then, despite my years in practice, I was an initiate to the complex story she was bringing to me. 'I know that this might be hard, Agnes, and I understand it will be painful and that also, there will be missing bits.' She interrupted quickly, 'I remember nothing, nothing. Absolutely nothing, Doctor, about any of it. I did not know, I really did not, did not, know I was pregnant.' She said the word with revulsion. She had let out a wail, 'No one believes me,' looking so helpless and lost.

'But it happens to other women.'

I can see so clearly now how working with Agnes woke me up from my slumber. I'd been sleepwalking through life, life with its vital senses. Agnes herself and our work together shocked me into more awareness of my own management of all that had been banished within myself and carried by learned protective behaviours. I guess, thinking now, that it was time for such management to be revised. Avoidance of intimacy was the most obvious way I had protected myself, but I was to learn more about the cost of this. Obsessionality was another, fixing on any form of distraction to run away from the fear of body sensations and feelings inside; sensations that were often accompanied by impossible feeling.

Memories. Such important memories of those years. The years leading up to the summer my life changed. I listen again to Berlioz, Symphony Fantastique and I hear the harp begin. An important memory arises: I am looking out onto my garden showing the earliest signs of the coming Spring with new life, white tips of snowdrops and crocus, bluebell shoots, magnolia buds forming, willow leaves budding. February is a hard dark month to me, and I am relieved to see signs that new life is about to emerge from the dark earth when March and April arrive. A wonderful resource, new life from the deep. As I sat watching Spring begin to arrive that first year of our work, I also realised that March was possibly the month when Agnes' child was conceived, three years earlier. The music also reminds me again about the aftermath of one session during that first year where Agnes and I had been inching our way around possible dates for her pregnancy. She was found on Salisbury Plain in October, so we were trying to explore what was happening to her in the seven or eight months preceding. From the research of Carole, we learned that Agnes admission was late October that the child was very small, most likely premature, and weighed just under four pounds. Agnes had been daring to look more at those early months of that year when she possibly conceived her child. But in this first year of our work together she had revealed very, very little about that time except that she had had to move in to live with her mother, a time of great difficulty and harshness.

On that day, after the session, I was playing that same Berlioz music. I was moving around my room as the violins took up the 1–2–3 rhythm and were joined by the harp. It always reminded me of the possibility of spring. As the music played, I noticed that Agnes had left her familiar cobweb scarf. She had told me that the scarf was really important to her, like a talisman. I was surprised then by her use of this word. Agnes was to continue to surprise me! The scarf came from Cracow. She wore it twisted around her neck and into her lap, her hands always playing with it. It was knitted, and made of fine pale grey wool, woven to look like cobwebs. But what I did then, spontaneously, without thought or consideration, was to pick up the scarf and feel it. I wound it in both of my hands and began to move around the room in a sort of primitive dance in time to the music. I loosened it as I danced so that I could see all the patterns and the light in between the cobweb shapes. Then I saw Agnes's face at the small window in my garden door. She had returned to collect the scarf once she realised she had left it. This Polish talisman was her protector. She wound it around her wrists, arms and hands; it often covered her mouth, but her whispers could still be heard through the webbing. I was to learn that it was her protector against attack.

She let herself in through the door. Her eyes were huge. We stood in silence, just as the music was reaching a crescendo. Still keeping eye contact, she stepped forward, her hands outstretched, and unwound one end of the scarf from my left hand and invited me, by a nod of the head and a graceful ballet movement, to join the dance. We waltzed very slowly around the room; the scarf stretched between us.

Berlioz waltzed on, his vibrations powerful, hopeful, spring-like, despite his being at the end of an unhappy love affair when he wrote it. After the music stopped, we held eye contact, the scarf marking a limp connection between us and a boundary to touching. She smiled a large, beautiful smile as did I. She then took the scarf from me, gathered it together to be wound around her body, bowed, smiled and left. The scarf had formed a shared umbilicus between us.

The thought came to me then that it would have been about the same time of the year when she conceived her child. It was to be a turning point in our work. An unnamed umbilicus coming three years after the actual conception of her child. Leading to a birth, for both of us.

Chapter 5

The way forward seemed to have arrived in the silent dance of that encounter. Within it there was the intention to join together spontaneously in an open exploratory way. Within the shared enjoyment of sound and the nonverbal movement of dance a glimpse of life, lived and unlived, was possible through sensation and feeling, without analysis. The unpacking, reflecting, naming and sharing were to come later. And infinitely slowly, at their own pace. This balance of communications led us to look together at Agnes's complex story with courage and imagination.

It also plunged me into times of deep regret for what I had repressed or rejected myself. But it did mean that I now had an opportunity to reflect again on my some of my own unlived internal life, which I had buried or taken for granted. It was startling to discover how much I too had run away from fertility on all levels, physical, emotional, psychological.

When my sister, Margaret, and I were 10 our parents were killed in a car accident on their way to Cornwall. It remains a time of deep confusion and horror. Both Margaret and I were on the edge of adolescence, beginning to ask more questions from matters previously taken for granted, to involve ourselves more in adult issues. We became orphans. My mother's brother, Gareth, took it upon himself to keep an eye on us during our holidays from boarding school. My images of him, our only remaining relative, are vivid. He was often embarrassed to speak with us and always in a hurry to get away having done his duty. I longed for information about my parents, who seemed to have been deeply private about all personal matters. It was Gareth who told me that my mother was in her forties when Margaret and I were born. She thought that she was having the menopause – Uncle Gareth coughed at this word – and she and my father had given up hope of having children. My mother did not discover she was pregnant until just a month before our birth, which was premature, as with most twins. She and my father were shocked, unprepared. They had just converted their cottage in Suffolk. There were no spaces for children. Despite her doctor's recommendation she go to hospital due to her age my mother decided on a home birth. She wanted to be like her cousin, who had given birth to three children at home, music playing, husband in attendance. It was 1955, my mother was old-fashioned and didn't trust hospitals. She wanted to be comfortable and look out onto her garden.

When I reflected on this, I wondered whether she had been an idealist, not comfortable with basic practicalities. She and my father had married late, having met in the same accounting office soon after the war ended. She was always good with numbers. Perhaps she imagined that her child would just slip out of her whilst she was watching the garden or doing her knitting. I remember both my parents being uncomfortable with matters of the body. They kept us at a distance.

It was the midwife, who was about to pack up after my birth, who noticed my mother grimacing realised that there was another baby trying to be born. Margaret emerged, tiny, fragile, only just breathing and we were all rushed to hospital, my mother bleeding badly. Margaret was so small she had to be intubated. My mother was in shock, and we both heard Gareth mutter on one occasion that our poor mother could not look at us for days. Margaret found this very painful.

I wondered what effect this could have on the newborn after those months growing inside. 'We were inconvenient, Maxie,' Margaret had said hotly one day when we were walking together on the Suffolk beach near the cottage that was now ours. Perhaps this was where my innate sense of my parents' apparent lack of interest in us stemmed from. I had always been concerned about how interesting we were to them and was eager to please them. 'Oh yes, Max, you've vowed to be a very good boy haven't you? No risk taking, no going near the hot sticky, stuff!' Philip again, dear, dear Philip.

Who were they, our parents? What were they like? I had so often wanted to know whether they thought of us on that last drive away, having left us with new carers for the weekend as they needed, apparently, some 'personal space' – a modern expression much used in the 60s and 70s. I learned later through reading the reports that my father had been driving and had swerved to avoid a collision as another car came racing around the corner ahead. The driver was young, an inexperienced driver and drunk. My father swerved to avoid this oncoming car and in doing so collided with a huge oak tree which shattered their skulls. This was a time before seat belts. The young driver survived. My parents' car was smashed. They died on impact. It had always felt so random, so unfair, so desperate. Our fate, Margaret and mine was sealed at that moment.

This was yet another memory, of such a deep loss so young, that became freshly awakened soon after seeing Agnes and listening to and resonating with her painful early history. As I watched her, I realised I shared with her the learned patterns of clenched jaw, raised shoulders, the habitual holding of breath and occasionally hyperventilation. I thought again about my tracing of the heart in the shower, and that just behind the heart was the vagus nerve, triggered and inflamed by assaults on our nervous systems. I 'knew' in my head that I had had to numb down body and emotion to manage after their deaths, carrying on, looking after Margaret, having to make all kinds of decisions. I was beginning to see these old hard learned patterns, habits, built from this time with fresh eyes. The events were too much for the nervous system of a 10-year-old lad.

Also, I was to learn from my studies that the traumas of many life events, including those of earlier generations could be passed down from one generation to another. My parents had survived the war, my father serving as an air force pilot; my mother was a weather forecaster. Their reticence with expressing feeling was a form of control from a time when control was sorely needed. No room for emotion on the battlefront. And who knew what they had seen or heard from friends especially friends who returned shattered some of whom hardly ever spoke again. And I had seen much of this, now called PTSD in the clinic for soldiers.

The impossible emotional burden carried by Agnes' Polish grandparents threatened and persecuted in war torn Poland, would seem to have been continued in the psyche and personality of Agnes' mother also. Agnes had been brought up in close range with so much unconscious material. It was as if forms of complex and often sudden and violent death were becoming more present in my therapy room during those hours with Agnes. As well as unlived life.

Gareth would take us to the park in South London,

where in spring the young cygnets played on the grassy edges of the lake and Margaret would rush ahead and dance around with them. Once we became adolescent, he decided he should try to tell us the facts of life. Periods, erections, sex, sex between men and women, pregnancy. He was even more embarrassed than usual, red faced. I remember being startled when he told me again, in between coughs, that when her periods stopped my mother thought she had started the menopause. We had just arrived at the lake; the swans and cygnets were gathering in excited groups and Margaret was already way ahead. The lake, shimmering in the spring air, was completely captivating and beautiful. A majesty within itself. But into this image of grace and innocence came the thought of one's mother, having periods! Too embarrassing! I did know by then what they were as Margaret had rushed to tell me one school exeat that she had 'started'.

But more challenging than periods was the idea of my parents having sex. My young self was jolted out of its familiar numbness. They rarely hugged each other let alone anything else. I remember not having many words for sex between men and women then. Whatever making love was about was far away. Those long grey days following their deaths were all one continuum, but here was something new. Maybe, I think now as I approach 65, they were closer to each other than I had imagined and had affection, indeed appetite for each other if at least they were having sex that led to conception. Through my numbness some excitement was kindled at the thought of them having a more vital physical time than I had been aware of in my 10 years of being with them. This was followed by anger – why didn't they show it, why weren't they able to show or teach me some of life's pleasures, or at least that pleasures were possible. And all this at a time of the swinging 60s and 70s. But of course, they were of the generation that held that permissive age in scorn. Scorn perhaps masking fear. But I had learned many forms of control since I was ten, so I had few words for feelings and had not ventured into verbal expressions, as had Margaret. Until Oxford and Frances I had no sense of the potency of sensual or sexual pleasure, nor dared to give expression to emotion.

I never wanted to be any trouble. I guess I feared being

judged 'bad', but why I should fear this is hard to fathom. But damn it, what times and experiments I missed out on! As an adolescent lad, could I risk having sex, experimenting, enjoying myself as other boys in my school boasted they did in the holidays. The answer was that, somehow, I couldn't. I watched Margaret go out and experiment over and over. She had found a release from tragedy in rebellion and intended just to let herself go. She goaded me frequently. But I couldn't, perhaps I had some omnipotent idea that I needed to be the strong responsible one in order to protect her. But it didn't work.

There is that familiar heavy feeling in my chest. I've always associated it with loss, impossible loss, perhaps loss for something I never actually had. A loss for what had never been able or allowed to be born. Like Agnes, she would carry that image always.

Thinking of all this I am reminded of another afternoon, when I was 14. Gareth had taken me out from school on an autumn term exeat and we were again walking in the nearby park. He had probably decided it was time to offer me more details about the physical difference between men and woman and what I might expect as I became a teenager. He didn't know Margaret! She had begun experimenting with boys and her own body years before, at age twelve, and told me all about it in lurid detail.

'I've seen other boys' thingy,' she told me confidently. We looked at each other. She was excited. 'It was standing up and he was stroking it.' She looked at me challengingly. 'Have you tried that, Maxie? Please tell, please tell me what it like.'

I was embarrassed, and ashamed. I probably blushed and stammered. I had not started experimenting with my own body. I was also probably frightened for Margaret, for what might happen to her being so out of control. Like the youngster with the car that killed our parents. She was living dangerously. My complete opposite. I had to stay strong and safe to help her. Even though I failed her in the end.

'Please, please, Margaret, we are too young ...' She interrupted me.

'I've had a go with mine, with my down below,' she said, looking at me out of the corner of her eye. 'I know where to rub.'

'With boys?' I asked, shocked.

'Oh no,' she laughed, 'I'm waiting for the right one, one with a good body, especially a good bum.' She had winked at me and rubbed her hands over mine. 'I wonder what Bob Dylan's is like?' She was clearly fascinated. 'But, Maxie, I've seen them at it, boys and girls and, do you know, boys and boys. It's weird isn't it, all that humping about like two great elephants.'

Maybe I was envious. What would it have been like if I'd been more courageous? After all, experimenting with one's body sexually is all part of growing up. But not, sadly, for me. Then. Sad, damn it.

Gareth was, as usual, embarrassed speaking to us about such matters in case we were upset, or just emotional. Margaret loved to tease him by asking pointed questions such as 'What happens if a man's thingy won't go in?' and he would try to avoid answering and hurry to get away. Where had she learned all this? How did she get to be so brazen and free? I was never to know. But perhaps, as the more cosseted child, she had more freedoms. Margaret. The conversations, the sharing we might have had! I fantasise that she would not have allowed me to become so emotionally and sexually repressed. She would have wanted to know when I had done it and how, wanted to see the woman I had my eye on and size her up on all fronts. Thinking about Agnes and her suffering brought back many memories of Margaret, and of what might have been. Margaret was allowed to be 'different'. She dared many new things in her short life, lived dangerously at times. I will always miss her.

She was so tiny when she was born, she lived in an incubator for several weeks. She was the almost-forgotten twin, the gift from God, my mother decided, and this was a story that I did know, that had been told to me many times, which was why we all had to be careful around her, me especially. The almost-forgotten twin became the miracle twin who lived despite being born so small and hardly breathing; the special one around whom we all had to be careful such was her fragility. I think now, how having been so overprotected she had had to rebel to release herself and become as daring as possible. Which she was. Out of that early glass-encased fragility, emerged a fiery volatility. A fiery volatility that helped her sensitive nature to survive our parents' deaths but took her to her own early death by her own hand.

I seemed to be reflecting back on all the parts of the jigsaw puzzle of the Agnes years, stimulated certainly by her proposed visit. In her note she said that she was well and wanted to see me again, because she had something to show me. As I reflect still on our sessions and conversations, I seem to be asking more questions about human vulnerability. The living presences of Margaret and myself of which my mother was unaware; life in potential only, like the child Agnes never knew was growing inside her; the child, my child that might have been with Frances. These themes, of the potential for new animate life, illustrate all that is possible for a human living consciously inside a human body. Sensation, feeling, thought and passion. I've always had a feeling of something missing.

I have to get up and walk around slowly as my heart is racing again. Over the years I've learned to respect these happenings. I think again of Philip, dying suddenly from a heart attack, alone in a field, his dog by his side. I wish I had been there.

Philip. He had had no symptoms physically and was fit. But he had been carrying around the suffering of many losses for most of his life. It's one thing to know about something and another to allow oneself to feel it and allow space around it. He taught me so much and so often his words return to me. I wished we had talked more. I wish he had been present during my therapy with Agnes and I wish he could have seen me now, a changed man, happier than I've ever been. And yes, dear friend, I have allowed the rough beast to be born!!

I take some mindful walking steps into the garden before leaning against the old oak. Philip had looked at me keenly several times as he pressed his hand against my chest and said, 'Is it all in there, Max? Your loneliness?' At the time I was surprised and had said of course not. He had smiled his wry Australian smile and said with such sadness, 'I'm lonely. I think this is the right word for it. I've always been lonely, and it's not to do with having other people in my life.' We were on one of our regular walks with Belle across the heath. 'What rough beast. What rough beast is slouching towards Bethlehem to be born?' He had looked at me, real pain in his blue eyes. I felt something in my chest then but had no words. So, I tried to be clever. 'You, an Aussie, reading Yeats!' I said. He did not pick up on that but continued to look serious. There was a long silence between us.

'Yes, me an Aussie reading Yeats. But that poem, it's all in there. Read it, Max, read it again. "The Second Coming" – shit, man, the pun on those words! Those Irish poets, Becket, Joyce, Yeats … God, they knew something. They could get under the obvious, into the hinterlands. They bloody knew about passion in all its glory and its devastation; and what happens when we bury it.'

I wasn't ready then, as I was later, and remain so to this day, to engage with more of the deeper meaning and place myself inside it. To take a risk. To find that beast slouching its way to be born … But his words touched me then and they do again now. I now know much more about what he meant. The loneliness he asked about and which was shared was the loneliness of living in a learned cocoon, unable to feel deeply, unable to take risk, express passion, to lose oneself in an embrace. The dynamic energy available in passion, particularly sexual passion, becomes bestial through repression. But the war is within oneself. A cold war indeed.

There have always been other people in my life but always at a distance. And I was never more alone than when I was married to Emily.

Chapter 6

I had studied basic anatomy and physiology during my training, and neuroscience much later. But nothing then related to what I began to read when I was seeing Agnes. What I read was a revelation, thrilling. I learned that all living forms – plants, insects, animals, humans – begin life in movement and continue to move as an expression of the life force that flows through them. In the beginning atoms and particles dance, they separate and then come together, and form molecules. Molecules come together to form cells. Cells form complex living creatures and plants. All are alive, moving, growing, taking their places.

Movement was the connecting principle involved in every aspect of life. Human movement begins within the fallopian tubes of a female body where the successful dance of meeting and penetration between sperm and ovum results in a tiny embryo which moves its way into the uterus. Its entire development depends upon movement, a perpetual flow of motions and gestures which shape the new being into form, into what will become the organs, muscles, blood supply, nervous system of a human body. I could sense and hear that dance, similar to the dance I had with Agnes and her scarf.

I noticed another kind of electronic buzz when I read that the first organ to begin to function in utero is the embryonic heart. It begins life as two interconnected tubes of primitive muscular tissue made by the cells at the top of the head. After reading this I remember standing in the shower and consciously tracing that journey from my own head to my heart, marvelling. What a mighty organ it was! I could hear Philip's voice: 'It's all there, dear friend, all there.' I could imagine him doing a playful dance, thrusting out his chest. 'Go for it, Max. Life – proper big-hearted, full-bodied life.'

Still in the shower I returned to connecting with the marvel that these original cells of the heart begin on the outside of the embryo in the place which will eventually become the forehead. The embryonic heart looks up and out. This head end of the embryo grows rapidly and at only 4 weeks after conception is drawn down towards the tail end in a deep C-shaped curve. With this gesture the developing heart is brought down and in, to the centre of the chest. The heart finds its home. It also brings with it some 40,000 neurons which send more information to the heart than the heart does to the brain. I found this phenomenal. There is a little brain in the heart, sensitive to all movement and the energy of communication.

After this I sat down and pondered on it all. How had I imagined the heart, my heart? Or had I limited the understanding of the heart to rational thinking? Had I been so caught up in notions of the physical heart, the pump that had gone wrong for Philip? Or had I tried to transcend the physicality of the heart and its wider meaning through seeking to be 'above' these physical things. Or to dismiss any imaginations of the heart as mere romanticism. I laughed at myself and bent forward to splash water all over my face and my ignorant head.

I laugh at myself now when I think of this again and how innocent I was, how unconscious. And now I understand that it's not either–or. In order to feel or know anything I know now that I must be properly inside a body, living there in as much fullness as possible.

And love, always seen as coming from the heart, had many, many different forms. I had known about, and I practised with bodhicitta, the awakened expansive heart of Buddhism capable of being with suffering, one's own and others, and extending compassion to oneself and to all living beings. And I will hold this dear always. But how much had it remained as an ideal rather than a felt sense living reality?

I remember having such deep ponderings then. I can see now that it was the beginning of a wonderful awakening. How much had I allowed these, - ideas, beliefs, body and mind awareness in my own human life? Had I included my own body and all its appetites? If I hadn't recognised it before, then here it is I thought as I reflected then. I 'knew' that human love had to include physical touch and sexual intimacy. I 'knew' that we were part of a family of other beings, animals, plants, insects, living with the elements of the earth, air, water. Interbeing. We live inside bodies, everything we are and express must come through this vehicle.

I remember thinking of Margaret, growing side by side with me, inside our mother in different uterine sacs. Did our heart cells develop and begin to beat at the same time? Probably not. Who were we for each other, gestating together within the same space? In life we were so very different from each other physically and emotionally and destined to take such different paths.

Over the years I'd learned to begin my daily exercise programme in the shower, stretching, standing on one leg and balancing, celebrating the gift of water on the top of my head. I often hummed a tune from a Rossini's Messe Solennelle as I counted 1–2–3–4, 1–2–3–4. Slow, melodic, moving in rhythm. I would think often about the beginning of the formation and pulsing of that great organ, the heart.

The dance with Agnes and the scarf awakened many avenues in our work and also in my own inner life. A few weeks after I was again standing in the shower, enjoying the feeling of the warm water falling all over my body. Again, I raised my hand to my head where the water cascaded, then brought it slowly across my brow, down to the throat and into the chest area where the heart resided. I realised I was consciously and physically tracing the journey of the heart cells that had been there for over 60 years, from the top of the head down into my chest. I then let my hand rest just to the left of my sternum and continued to relish the fluidity of the water. It was thrilling.

Later, I sat down to play Chopin again. So poignant, wistful. Perhaps a melodic yearning for the new life spring might bring.

Perhaps this yearning was what had always been in my own heart but had gone unrecognised. I remembered again Philip patting me on the chest, close to the heart, Carole also. And Chopin, with a Polish background like Agnes, spent most of his life in Paris. I'd read that, in preparation for his own death, he had arranged for his heart to be smuggled past the Russians by his sister so that it could be buried with his family in Warsaw. He sent his heart back to Poland – what did this say?

After I'd read more and felt better informed about conception, I had waited for what felt like the right time to ask Agnes about the possible time of the conception of her own child. She had been found in late October and her daughter had most probably died inside her, to be born so very tiny and premature.

But our moving in to discuss the six or seven months earlier, and how conception might have happened, was much more difficult. We had drawn a blank for many months. 'I remember nothing, nothing,' she said over and over, clearly distressed.

Memories again - It was just a few weeks after the dance with the scarf, the scarf I have called the umbilicus, and I was expecting Agnes for her session. There was a stirring of anticipation in me, unusual.

It was late April. Bulbs, flowers. The sound of the goldfinch, the smiling faces of the celandine opening in the sun, the earth's heart beating after the slow waiting of winter. Pulsating. We sat together, me with my recent reading about the movement of the heart cells in utero about to mention the spring, but she gets there before me. 'Chopin', she says quietly having heard me play, '1–2–3–4 ... his love of spring, don't you think, Doctor?'

I remember smiling at our shared connection. 'What is it about this time that you enjoy most?'

She had beamed, 'Everything coming into life. Bulbs pushing up from the winter earth; the nests of fledglings; I've already heard the skylark even here in South London.' She had hesitated: 'There's a mallard duck on our local pond hiding under the reeds with her newly hatched chicks. The drake scuttles around finding food for them.'

I remember saying 'The pulsing of new life,' and put my hand on my heart.

She drew her breath inwards and looked down.

I took a risk: 'Anything else you remember about spring?'

Her head bowed. 'You mean that spring.'

'Yes. That spring. Three years ago, Agnes,' I said quietly.

Silence.

I took another risk: 'What do you remember Agnes, I seem to recall that you were still living with your mother? At that time three years ago?'

'I know where you're going with this.'

'Let's take it slowly. Agnes.' She twists and turns. 'We need to be brave enough to go there.'

I kept the difficult silence for a while and then said, 'Would you rather we spoke of the summertime, three years ago. Would this be easier?' I imagined that her daughter would have been growing inside her that summer, moving day and night. She cut into my sentence ...'I think you know, I had to go back and live with my mother for a while.' Silence.

'I remember you telling me, Agnes, not long after we met. And that it was a very, very difficult painful time for you.'

She turned toward me. 'That Christmas, I did mention it to you once I think... My tenancy came to an end because I couldn't afford the rent increase.' She was twisting the scarf more intensely around her hands.

'When did you return?'

'That winter. That horrible winter. I'd had a sort of breakdown ...' she gulped and began to speak in more detail about that time. 'It started with a fall ... a bad fall ... my hands were injured when I tried to protect myself. Anna and Mark were spending six months in New Zealand, otherwise I think they would have taken me in....' She paused, muttering... 'I'm so ashamed, so ashamed...' She was bent right over, and I could only just hear her. I leaned forward as unobtrusively as possible not wanting to interrupt her, but not wanting to lose a word. She took a deep breath. 'Then I got pneumonia and couldn't do much work.' She spread her now elegant hands out before her.

'I've always been self-employed. I was working all hours at all kinds of menial jobs to make ends meet ... I couldn't teach piano because of my hands ... No money.' She looked deeply sad. 'Snow on the streets. It was so cold ...' She wrapped her coat and shawl around her adding, 'on all levels.'

'Agnes', I leant forward as I spoke. 'I am so sorry, so sorry for what you've had to go through.'

'Thank you, thank you, Doctor Max. You are... kind.'

'You've spoken of your mother being quite a bitter woman, pretty hard on you.'

Silence. She was becoming more and more bent over and her eyes were closed.

'Yes,' she said quietly. 'Yes. She took me in. I suppose that's a good thing, isn't it? But she viewed me as a failure. I'd failed to maintain my independence.'

'That's sad.'

She shrugged, 'I have thought about it quite a bit since. And spoken to Anna who's been quite shocked by my mother's... attitude.'

There was a long pause. 'It's her past. For her it's all about success or failure, nothing in between.' She gave a huge sigh. 'Her parents, my grandparents, were Polish. They managed to escape from the Nazis in Cracow in 1944. They were poor and sad, apparently always sad. That much I have gathered. But she's told me little.' There was a pause. Her story was beginning to unfold. 'They lived in an old Nissen hut in a small village in Essex. My grandmother had been a concert pianist in Poland and now had to take in sewing and my grandfather did odd menial jobs.' She paused. 'My mother was born in 1947, here in England. She was a very late arrival for my grandmother.' Agnes gulped, looking down, saying very quietly: 'as I was for my mother.' This was really hard for her. 'My grandmother died in childbirth, and I think that my mother was brought up by other Polish families and at times looked after by some English families also.' She gave another huge sigh. 'I don't know what happened to my grandfather. She always looks the other way when I ask and says, 'leave it all alone, Agnes, you've been lucky.' She was continuing to twist the scarf intensely around her hands. 'But she never has told me who my father was or is.' Another huge sigh. 'You can see our history, Doctor, can't you? The patterns.'

The quality of silence was profound and sad. I found myself thinking of the mothers of these births, mine and Margaret's, Agnes' mother, both to women on the edge of physical change in mid-life. Both possibly ambivalent about giving birth.

She began twisting the grey scarf again, around and around her hands, looking into the distance. 'Mind you, I've not spoken to her for ages. I've stopped trying. I imagine she won't want to have anything to do with me now, after all that's happened.'

'I'm so sorry, Agnes.' I ask, 'Does she live in London?'

'Yes. She still lives where I grew up. Brixton.'

'Say more about what it was like?' I felt that she had

so much more to explore here and wanted her to continue. She clearly did not remember telling me some of these facts earlier.

'Then do you mean, three years ago?'. She laughed a brittle laugh. 'Hard. I was just a nuisance to her always. I curtailed her freedom. She couldn't wait until I left home at 18. She started dating again after I left and by then she was in her 60s.' She remained looking down. 'Nothing ever lasted. She'd probably just been dumped by her latest fling and there I was again, curtailing her.' She looked up, 'she's an angry woman. Never managed to live fully. I've always thought she was trapped in her ancestral past, but she would never speak of it. I never met any of my Polish relatives, if indeed I have any, nor do I know anything about their history.' She continued to wind the scarf round and round her hands, such tension in it. I felt heavy-hearted. I knew again there was so much more here and hoped it would reveal itself in time. 'She's 73 now.'

Her tone was resigned. I was intrigued. We had moved away from the subject we needed to home in on, but something else was arriving.

The scarf, I smiled. Poland. I nodded toward the scarf.

'You said that the scarf came from Poland. From Cracow I remember?' I asked.

She raised the scarf to her lips. 'Anna and Mark, Anna's fiancé then, returned from their trip that February and they bailed me out one weekend during that dreadful winter, bless them. They could see how hard it had been for me living there. It was a surprise for my birthday. March 5th. They had done quite well financially and booked us a weekend. Anna could see I was … I was struggling, at my mother's.'

'I'm so happy to hear that you have kind friends.' I said. She looked down. 'What can you remember about Cracow?' She was silent. 'Do you have photographs?' I asked.

She shook her head. Then suddenly looked up and said: 'Anna thought it would help me, to know more about my history, to understand more about why my mother was as she was. Anna is so kind.' I waited to see whether she might say more.

She took a deep breath, before saying quietly, 'Anna has photographs and kept a diary. But, but, I've not been able to look at them.' She took another deep breath. 'Not yet. But I will, I know I must. It's time isn't it.' Her eyes were full of both fatigue and determination. 'Not looking. Not wanting to be reminded. As if that will mean that it never happened.' She sighed deeply. Then folded her hands quietly. 'But I'm not like my mother. I do know that.' We sat together with all these revelations. Then she said, 'The child. I never saw her. My child. A daughter, they did tell me that. I'm starting to wish I had. She would be two and a half now.'

I was surprised by her sudden shift of subject and her recognition. I wondered if she might begin wondering what kind of mother she might have been as she had been speaking about her own mother and always feeling a nuisance to her. But this was for another time.

'Did you have the opportunity?' She remained looking down. 'The first hospital, emergency department, they seemed to get it that I'd been in some kind of trauma. Honestly, Dr Maxwell, I've so little memory, so little.' There was a long pause. ' Except that one or two were kind. Really kind.' Her eyes filled with tears. She said in a whisper, 'That was amazing, really amazing ...'

I remembered that one of the reasons she had been drawn to Salisbury Plain was that she had memories of being taken there and had received real kindness from another.

'Yes, indeed,' I said warmly, 'kindness is one of the most important offerings there is.'

She looked suddenly wary, frightened. I was to learn much more about this wariness as time went on. Then, hanging her head, saying in a whisper, 'I've seen people being kind to each other. Real kindness. But it's not been for me. Perhaps I don't deserve kindness.'

This shared reality touched me to my core.

Chapter 7

The following week Agnes arrived early and looked through the glass window of my garden door. I was listening to Fauré's Siciliana. I beckoned for her to come in.

It was becoming an accustomed ritual; if I was playing something when she arrived, as soon as she came in, she'd start to hum or to move her body in tune with the music. Sometimes she would play some notes on the piano, her body leading the way. I would stand and watch her in silence. We did not use words for these times.

Agnes sat down, looking thoughtful. 'Good music for this day. Simple, direct.' She smiled. 'I've had a dream.'

She had written it down on a single piece of paper. She had not taken up the idea of keeping a journal I had suggested early on. She was living each moment, as if fleeting. It was the first dream she had recorded and brought, and I felt a sense of relief. I had asked her often about dreams, but she had shaken her head and looked down. I was still holding the image of the dream of her child she told me about at our first session: 'She comes to me in my dreams – "I wanted to land. To land with you."'

She had hesitated before unfolding the piece of paper. 'In the dream I am walking through the park near where I live.' She looked up. 'There's a lake there and I often sit as close as I can to its life, watching the movement of the water, and water life; nature arriving and changing throughout the year. The leaves changing colours with the seasons, the sounds, the lonely call of the owl in the hush of dusk … So wonderful.' Her eyes glowed. 'I've been watching the moorhens. The mother has been sitting on her eggs, just occasionally peering out from the reeds. The eggs have now hatched, and I sit watching the little ones, their jerky early movements, so quick …. The father moorhen scuttles around in protective mode, squawking. The Mum huddles in with them inside the reeds. They are so … so fresh, immediate, so active … so brave … such great parents …'

She hesitates before returning to the dream. She takes a deep breath. 'A huge hand appears, a human hand, white with long painted, red, fingernails … It grabs them, the baby moorhens. One by one … One by one it picks them off.' She shakes her head, tears in her eyes. 'It flings them far. I can't watch.' She puts her hand to her chest and takes some slow breaths. 'But when I look again, one is left. Her Mum has grabbed her to her body and together they find refuge in a clump of deep reeds … The father moorhen scuttles nearby making lots and lots of squawking noises.'

We sit with the feeling of this dream.

She shrugs. 'Obvious, isn't it. My history, it's as if it's all inside me. My mother's parents and their families were threatened and picked off by the hand of the Germans just because they were Polish, and most probably Jewish I don't know, but so so vulnerable. They were flung far and wide. My grandparents managed to get smuggled here, they arrived with nothing. Their history, what they had seen… I don't suppose they ever spoke of it and my mother was born a couple of years after her parents arrived here when my grandmother was in her 40s, and then her father, my grandfather disappeared. That's all I know, all I've been able to gather from the odd, and difficult conversations with my mother. My mother's birth … just post-war, possible new life for my grandparents dashed and my mother, born into death. The death of her mother, the disappearance of her father. No family connections, no easy community. Not much kindness there I guess doctor.' She sat back in her seat looking sad. 'As far as I can gather, she was brought up by a mixture of Polish and some English people in the village. There's always been a bitterness in her, but she will never speak of her early life.'

'It's a very sad history, Agnes.' I did feel deeply sad.

'It's as if she's always lived as an oppressed victim. Ready to be picked off by a predator at any moment.' There was a long pause. 'Like my dream,' she said quietly.

There was a long pause between us.

'She will never discuss anything about my father. Maybe he disappeared, or maybe he never knew.' She wept. 'And I never knew did I? I just didn't know. My mother,' she said after a long pause. 'She's kept such a spikey self, as if she has to be on the attack against all, against all who could invade. Even I could be seen like that at times, getting in her way, restricting her freedom.' There was another long pause and she repeated,

'So she's kept a spikey self.'

I noticed how profound, under the sadness of the content, was the understanding in this comment. The vast collective weight of a huge ancient historical sadness filled my room.

'I've often wondered if perhaps my grandmothers' husband had left, or died in the two years after they arrived here; and that my mother was conceived by someone else. Which would mean that the man who had braved it over to England with all that Polish history was not her biological father. Which is possibly why my mother never felt connected.' She looked down. 'But then he too disappeared before she could have known him.' She gave a big sigh. They must have been so vulnerable. Some people are kind to refugees, but some are definitely not.'

We just sat together sharing the painful truth in her words. As I was pondering on this more, she said, 'I've not been able to research into any Jewish heritage. It's just too painful. But it makes no difference, does it? I came from an historically oppressed group of humans who became victims to oppressive evil persecutors simply because of genes. We don't really know much do we about the nature of freedom, what it means between human beings.' Another pause in some of the longest, most reflective sentences she had uttered. 'Perhaps we all have to learn what freedom really means.' Big sigh. 'But it's not straightforward, is it? It's all a great journey ... And, and ... history repeats itself,' she said quietly.

Then, before I could say anything, 'But, but, here,' she looked up at me, her blue eyes suddenly bright, 'in this room, the way I was brought here through fate. Here is where the pattern can be challenged, changed even?'

I was moved. I noted the phrase 'history repeats itself' and wondered where this might take us in relation to the child she conceived. Victim and persecutor. Was Agnes raped? Many of her ancestors might well have been raped in one of the camps. Could it have been one of her mother's lovers?

'Indeed, Agnes,' I said. 'Indeed, it can be, and this is our work. We cannot change the past, but we can decide to choose our attitude toward it.'

She smiled. 'To choose what has already chosen us. Yes.' I was impressed. 'It's what Carole says,' she said.

I smiled inwardly. This was something Carl and I had spoken of in relation to his early life and fate, his time in the army. His longing to be more attuned to feeling, to the qualities we tend to associate with femininity. I was pleased that these shared ideas, indeed possible choices, could act as living philosophies, and be passed on to others.

'Perhaps my mother has never known kindness, or gentleness.'

She shrugged and remained looking sad, and I felt it also. Whilst acknowledging the tragedy and suffering in so much of Agnes' history I was pleased that some real feeling connection was arising within her and spoken of for the first time. I was impressed with her insight. I was about to ask her more about history repeating itself, but she spoke first.

'The poor moorhen ...' and looked up brightly, 'but there was one life left, a newly born life, wasn't there, Doctor? And this little chick had two parents.'

Perhaps encouraged by the dream and the hope in it, Agnes brought her friend Anna to the next session so that we could share the events of that early spring weekend in Cracow three years ago. Anna brought photographs that Agnes did not remember seeing before. She held her scarf to her face as a guard. Anna was gentle and helpful. The first photograph showed the three friends, Anna and her fiancé, now husband Mark, together with Agnes arriving at their beautiful small hotel, possibly once a home for a Polish family in the old part of Cracow. Agnes nodded, suddenly looking frightened.

'I only brought a few photos to begin with,' said Anna quietly. She turned toward Agnes. 'We will go slowly, Aggie, OK? Remember the moorhen dream and the close protection the mother hen offered her little one and the father moorhen scuttling around guarding outside the reeds. You have that now. We're the family that little part of you needs. We're here to help you.' Anna turned to the second photo, 'Here's one just after we arrived. A happy photo. Do you remember sitting in the market square and hearing the bugler?' Agnes shook her head.

I made a note of this as sound had always been so important to Agnes. Perhaps she had had to turn this sense off in Cracow.

'We had fantastic coffees and the sun shone wonderfully for March!'

Anna looked toward me, wanting to explain. 'Mark had been reading up about St Mary's Basilica. On the top of the church tower a trumpeter sounds a bugle call every hour, ever since 1241 and fears of Tartar invasion ... to warn the inhabitants.'

It seemed then as if Agnes was shrinking into her scarf. Anna continued to hold her arm around her and eventually Agnes dared to look down at the photograph. She closed her eyes and whispered, 'Is that where we went when we can back from ... you know.'

There was a pause within which it was as if we were all holding our breath.

'Oh, Agnes!' Anna sobbed. 'Yes, indeed.' She took a deep breath. 'Dearest, we should never have gone there. It frightened you so much. It frightened all of us.' She looked up at me. 'This photograph was taken on our first morning, we had just arrived and were enjoying the market square.' She took a deep breath and held Agnes' hand tightly. Her voice was quiet, serious. 'St Mary's was also the place where we went to pray and ask for blessings. It was after a visit to Auschwitz. When we planned our Cracow visit Agnes had insisted that we visit both camps, Auschwitz and Birkenau. Mark and I were uncertain, but it felt important for Agnes. We went there on our last day.'

Agnes seemed to be disappearing into her chair.

Anna continued. 'She was so very keen to understand more about her family. She knew that her grandparents had had to flee from the German Nazis. They were probably part of a Jewish family, and they managed somehow to get smuggled into the UK on a fishing boat. There were other family members, aunts, cousins, who did not survive. They died in the camps at Auschwitz–Birkenau, and also at Treblinka as far as she could discover. Agnes had just begun to do some research as best she could, but her mother is not at all forthcoming.' She paused, looking uncertain. 'I'm not sure how much you already know, Doctor...'

Agnes had by then buried herself in the scarf. There was a complete silence. I felt stunned. Anna looked concerned, hesitant.

'You see, she had started reading more, reading about Poland and the German occupation. Reading about the persecutions, about ordinary people being rounded up all over Poland. They were promised they would be taken to safe houses. But they were transferred to the camps and then sent to their deaths, extermination.' She was looking at Agnes as she was speaking. 'There is a book, called Bearing Witness by Bernie Glassman who had led post-war retreats there, aimed at healing. We had all read it, Mark and I as well. It's very moving, and it's also...not sure if this is the right word...hopeful...' She looked sad. 'We read it when Agnes started talking about wanting to know more about her Polish ancestors who had most likely perished in the camps there.'

Agnes, still enclosed in her scarf, was silently watching Anna with her huge eyes as she spoke, so earnestly, wanting to explain, for me, for all of us, to understand.

'The book, the ideas, the offerings, they were all so inspiring. I guess we thought we could all do the same. Bear witness to horrific things that happened to live vulnerable human beings. Find healing, pray for the Jewish people, for Agnes' Polish relatives and for the horrors of that time.' She paused, her gaze still on Agnes. 'We were idealistic, I can see now. No one can know the impact of these terrible places on their nervous systems, can they? We've lived in peace, it's impossible to know, to imagine how cruel, how persecutory, humans can be to each other. But at Auschwitz–Birkenau you see it all.' Anna took a deep breath. The atmosphere in my room was tense, and painful. 'All, in every small detail. It's a terrible place, to see, to be present with photographs and names, with the events … We had no idea of the impact on us, our feelings, our bodies, our nervous systems.' She looked down, clearly troubled. 'We were idealistic,' she repeated softly, 'idealistic Doctor.' She turned again closer to Agnes. 'Dear Aggie, I am so, so sorry we let you go there.' She turned to me, 'We had no idea of the shock it would cause her'.

I was startled. And intrigued. The paradox, the weekend of nourishment away from the bleak winter with her mother to which Agnes was invited so generously, became a weekend that touched an ancestral past that would lead her into acute distress and eventually deep psychological work.

I also had been impressed by the work of Bernie Glassman and read his book 20 years ago. I was impressed by his understanding of the potential for healing through the power of bearing witness, and many of these reflections had influenced my own work. I was also moved that this subject should appear once more in my work and encounters. And here, with Agnes, there was much need for healing on many different levels.

Anna began speaking again. 'It is a terrifying and brave place, today, carefully, sensitively presented, if one can say such a thing about such a place. There is an atmosphere of hush, of care...' Her voice dropped. 'It chills the blood seeing what Hitler's soldiers actually did, day by day, like running a business. To see evidence of the actuality,' she waved her hands, 'is completely different from words. There was absolute silence on our bus on the way back and we'd all been chatting on the way there.' She was holding both of Agnes' hands now. She turned to her. 'The doctor needs to know, dearest Agnes, he needs to know what traumas you have been through that have changed you, traumatised your poor body so that you have such little contact with it.'

I smiled at Anna's understanding. Agnes was still immobile in the chair under her scarf.

Anna held her gaze to Agnes, her face so full of feeling, of concern. 'We all got off the bus and went straight to the church and lit candles. We prayed for all those lost souls. We prayed for the living, for ourselves. We prayed for all Agnes' relatives. We prayed that there might be peace with all people, not divisions. The silence in the church was profound.' She looked into Agnes face, now peering out from the scarf. 'Do you remember any of this, Agnes?'

She shook her head. It felt too soon, all too soon.

After they had left, I sat in silence. Stunned. Here was something huge in Agnes' ancestral history and in her experience three years ago, at the time of year her child was most likely conceived. It felt as if the only thing she could do after being in the atmosphere of such wilful violence and persecution, all the death that was part of her ancestry, was to put everything of vital life on hold, suspended; her body, feelings, thoughts, and live on automatic.

But at the same time something new had been trying to gestate within her in the shape of her child. A new life that was to remain unlived physically, but which brought her into contact with different people interested in change and healing.

I went back to her first words when we met – 'How could I not know she was living inside me?' The sentence itself revealed a questioning self, the one we were currently engaged with. A questioning self I hoped would bring not just answers but a greater acceptance of all that she had come into life with. I also thought again of the paradox Agnes carried. Life and death, all at once. And life on what terms? And then there was guilt, which I recognised and shared with her. And the power of guilt, particularly guilt that seems to enter us in early life, unconscious guilt. It is guilt for something we could not possibly be guilty for. For events way beyond our conscious awareness or control which happened before our birth, or in very early life before we were able to have choice. And yet we experience it as if it were a fundamental truth.

This guilt, which I often call magical guilt, can threaten anything potentially creative inside us. It's as if we must pay for any gifts and good fortune we may have. Or, if we accept our life freely, allow our natural gifts and any new life to flourish, it's as if we are dancing on another's grave.

Chapter 8

After the session where she had come with Anna and the photographs, Agnes cancelled, leaving a short message on my answerphone. 'I just can't, Doctor Maxwell, I can't. Sorry.'

I sat and allowed my own feelings of disappointment to be present rather than reply to her on automatic, saying something formal and professional, understanding about how hard it was to reveal matters that were so painful for her. I did feel that we were on to something really important, which was still a mystery and needed time. And I was curious once more about the nature of my own involvement, about what did all this mean for me beyond professional reality. Of course, said an inside voice, as a therapist you are always involved, silly bugger. But with Agnes it was more. I felt as if I had allowed our emotional difficulties and blocks, and the energy between us to open something in me which I could not yet name. I was aware of our similarities, our sensitivity to past things that we had, as far as each of us knew, successfully buried. I didn't want her to leave just yet when so much was unresolved, but I was concerned about my motivation, that I wanted to see her again for my own reasons, which were as yet unclear.

I left a message for her, expressing understanding at the difficulty of revealing matters that were so painful; and that I would keep her space open for her. She could contact me whenever she was ready.

I didn't know how long I might wait, or if I would ever see her again, and I felt very sad. Sad for Agnes, and sad for myself. I realised later that my own sadness could be related to an old one, a disappointment that just as I might have touched on some new life for myself it was taken away. Like with Frances.

But a few weeks later she left another message and came to her session, this time with Carole. She looked brighter, something in her eyes. Carole was protective and stroked her arm, comforting her.

'Carole said I should come. I should continue, however difficult it might be.' She looked shy.

'That's really courageous Agnes,' I said. 'We can take our time.'

I leant forward, wanting to engage her. 'You had a huge shock last time you were here. We will go slowly and let your body lead the way.'

She smiled. 'Yes, exactly,' turning toward Carole. 'That's what you said too, isn't it.'

She stood up and began to show me some movements and postures, stretching her arms forward and back, patting the insides and outsides of her arms slowly. Carole looked on approvingly. Then she stood tall in the middle of the room and placed her hands over her abdomen, smiling. Carole watched fondly. She raised her hands to the sky and then allowed them to float gently down her body.

'I'm washing, cleansing my body,' she said, her eyes sparkling. 'I'm cleansing my body with golden light. Carole has been teaching me qigong.'

'We've just started classes at the clinic,' said Carole, explaining. 'It felt a good idea and Agnes has taken to it really well.'

We watched Agnes making more movements, her hands turning over each other slowly up and down, passing over the organs of her body. Head, brow, throat, heart, stomach and root. It was similar to what I had begun doing in the shower before my daily exercises. I was fascinated by the synchronicity.

She sat down and tears fell. She shrugged her shoulders. 'But I still can't remember anything, Doctor. Why can't I? If I can learn a new skill – if my body can help me learn a new way of being with it, why can't it tell me more, indicate somehow … I want to remember, I really do, just remember…' She slapped her thigh, hard.

Carole took her hand and said 'No, no, we go gently into the dark night, Agnes.'

I was touched then by their fondness for each other, and the trust Carole had obviously inspired in Agnes.

'You've made a wonderful start, Agnes, you have let your body lead the way with sound, with birdsong and music – remember dancing with the scarf? And it has definitely allowed you to have many more reflections of your life and your way of being. Trust it. Now you are learning something of the energies that we can engage with that are interrelated with our bodies through qigong and sharing it with others.' I turned toward Carole, 'And it seems you also have a companion, which is wonderful.'

'Yes! And she's been through such dreadful stuff also,' said Agnes, looking towards Carole.

I was aware then of this conversation becoming something of a threesome and felt slightly unnerved. I was not sure why at the time. But I noted it. Where did I belong in it all?

'You're being really courageous, Agnes. The qigong is a brilliant start, continue practising without expectation. Let your body lead the way, freely.' I thought for a few moments. 'If anything unusual comes to you, write it down, like you did with the dream...you might even decide to begin writing in the journal, don't judge, just write whatever arises, no matter how strange you may think it. It could be a fleeting feeling, an image, any form of memory from any time.'

She nodded, as did Carole, leaning toward her. 'Everything is linked,' she said.

I looked at Agnes keenly, wanting to engage her without Carole.

'I've thought more about the sharing we had when Anna came, the photographs. That last day in Cracow ...'

She shuddered and folded her arms around her chest, sinking into the chair. She looked at Carole. Then back at me. 'Don't ...'

I felt I had to be firm. 'You were traumatised by that visit on that last day. You went there wanting to know more about your family history which is brave. And you had a huge shock. You had no words to speak of what you had seen and the effect it had on you because it was unspeakable. The wounds of your ancestors were laid bare.'

I felt they were then both listening and was relieved. I leaned back, not wanting to be preacherly but wanting to pass on well researched information which I felt was my duty as a professional.

'Apologies for all this technical stuff, but it is really important – for all of us! Carole has heard it all before, from me and from the army!'

Carole nodded, solemnly. 'I know you need to give

us another little lecture, Doctor Max, Sir!' she said, her eyes teasing. 'Hope it won't turn into a full lecture!'

I turned to Agnes. 'So, this is just information. When we are threatened, by forces much greater than ourselves, bigger, powerful forces, internal or external, our nervous system takes charge. I know I've said it a few times, but I will continue to remind us – all of us, me included, that our bodies lead the way, Agnes.' I smiled, 'Believe me, I'm still working on it! When we are in deep shock we move into fight, flight or freeze mode. It's what we all do, all of us, Agnes. You could not fight or run away from the reality you saw and felt that day at Birkenau. You froze. Whatever memories and associations were touched then are still inside you in some form but have no words yet. Your body is carrying that experience. Over time we will, together–' I looked at Carole as I said this, 'together we will help you find the words. Finding words that match feelings in the body alongside an attitude of kindness helps us release them. They've been stored there and waiting for ….'

'Open Sesame,' whispered Carole, 'Open Sesame … I know … I've been there.' Tears were in her eyes.

There was a good silence, all of us taking in the words.

Agnes voice sounded choked. 'It's so hard to imagine that. It feels a long, long way away.'

'But not impossible, Agnes' said Carole softly.

'So, so … you're saying that if I, if I can find the words that release something only my body remembers, if I can, I would understand?'

I nodded. 'You then have the opportunity to find understanding, and also forgiveness wherever it is needed.'

'Are you, are you also saying – it's not my fault all this.' She swept her hands over her abdomen. I could see it, the idea, was a wonder to her. I nodded, Carole also. 'So, it doesn't mean I'm bad.' She whispered to herself, looking down. Then, 'I'm allowed to live….'

I was startled, concerned. I leant towards her and said quietly, 'You are allowed to live dear Agnes, keep saying this to yourself. This is your life to claim, for yourself. What happened is deeply, deeply sad, but does not mean you are bad.'

She looked up, looked across at Carole, and then at me,

breathing in and out very slowly. 'Thank you.'

After another pause, Carole signalled to Agnes' pocket.

'Oh yes, I nearly forgot. We, we've been writing poetry together'. She looked mildly anxious. 'I brought some, Carole said I should. Here it is.'

She separated her hand from her scarf and went into one of the deep pockets in her loose jacket and pulled out a small notebook with its own pencil. So, she had taken up the idea of a journal after all! It looked new, perhaps Carole had encouraged her to buy it for this purpose. When I saw her as Carl, he kept a journal all the time and brought it each week. 'It's my keepsake,' he said many times.

Agnes took some deep breaths and read slowly:
'The wild-eyed child awakens.
Afraid.
She does not know how to go step by step.
She whispers to those who might hear:
I'm too small.
They can still get me.
Slowly I bargain with my sad trifles
in the basement of the psyche.'
We all sat and let the words resonate.
'That is a beautiful poem, Agnes. Beautiful.'
She smiled, as did Carole, who stroked her arm again.

'It says so much. But just let us for now simply stay with the words and see how we feel as they land with us. Read it to us again, will you?'

She lifted the paper and read again, slowly. We all listened.

'Thank you,' I said quietly.

After a while she said again in a hesitant voice: 'So all this happening - it doesn't mean I'm bad.'

Carole and I sat with her, our faces smiling encouragement.

'You are not bad, Agnes'.

Her face creased with pain. 'But I was. Inside,' she pressed near her heart, 'inside I know I was bad after that visit.'

Later, after they had left, I think again about Agnes and Carole, meeting, learning qigong and writing poetry.

I remember being both pleased for their creativity and at the same time unnerved. I even wondered whether Carole was in some way trying to control her as her mother had done. She was certainly challenging me through her teasing glances and raised eyebrows. I noticed a certain tension and fear in my abdomen. And I wondered, is this all OK – two patients getting together whilst I am still seeing one of them. I had then laughed at myself. Was I being overcautious and formal? Was I even jealous? I could hear Philip saying, 'Let it go, man, you're such a stuffed shirt.' Did I wish I had more of Carole's courage – to go into battle as a man and get honoured for war services? Then allow a longing to live as a woman to be honoured, and now giving back some of what he had learned along the way, helping people with their internal battles with their bodies.

This was a time when I was learning to let go properly, to go with the unseen and welcome in the unexpected. I was learning much more about the struggle and paradox of living as consciously as possible within a human body, with all its history, its memory and its gender.

Again, those first words of Agnes come back to me – 'How could I not know she was living inside me?' They remind me of all that I have learned and practised since we met. It is mostly just sitting and noticing, truly allowing all the discomforts, pains to arise, just as they are, not overthinking or analysing. I can let memories that I thought long gone, even dead, arise and stay. I can welcome them in their aliveness. It's as if they've been waiting for me to notice them and begin a new relationship with them. Just sitting and noticing, kindly, is all that is needed now, allowing these gifts of body memory to rise. And to do this with an intention of acceptance and kindness. The learned responses that lead us to avoid any awareness of living in a body because of the painful truths it carries and can offer up is profound. So many of us learn the habit of running past what our body might be telling us in its muscles, aches and pains, tensions, habits. There sems to be an epidemic in our Western world with its rush to get it done, do it now or else attitudes. Don't feel, just get on with it. And the 'or else.' How little we get to explore the 'or else' so that we might have more freedom from the driver. Freedom to choose. But no, get on, get on … just take a pill, keep going … Just take a pill. Get on, get on.

It was to take Agnes and I considerable time of going really slowly before she could tolerate the conscious awareness of how much her body and nervous system had carried since her childhood. And the memories it awakened. For Agnes, emotional and physical traumas from her early life meant that she could not allow sensations and feelings to rise, for what could she do with them? They had never had safe passage.

'Stop bothering me,' was one of the many messages. 'You're just a nuisance.' 'Why don't you grow up.' 'Get out of my sight.'

She had to be guarded, on alert, her head always leading the way into any everyday activity, illustrated by her 'heron' way of walking. She had learned such survival skills so skilfully that allowed her to be fiercely independent, and to take charge of her life. She had sometimes even had to bail out her mother financially, rescue her from inappropriate relationships, from being drunk. And she had had to shrink away from her mother's rages and criticism for she had no reserves within which to find an answer. She received no thanks, just 'it's alright for you,' spoken with the voice of envy. She learned to play down what she had, what she could do. And other than music, pleasure was hard to find, let alone accept. Her return every day to the solace of music, listening and playing, was her great joy.

There was also the startling realisation brought to me by a colleague – to be pregnant, a life growing inside you, was a potential challenge for a woman's body and many adjustments hormonally were going on all the time. It could also be a disconcerting experience for anyone as their bodies were being challenged. Each day different as the foetus grows, organ by organ, limb by limb. But I also knew from my reading, and from Agnes, that she, and many other women had no awareness of any kind that she could be pregnant. I also thought many times about the shock it must be to be giving birth when all you had was what you thought was an upset stomach.

To this day I still make that movement from the top of my head into the centre of my chest marking the original journey of the heart cells. I've continued to imagine a heart growing cell by cell inside a tiny embryo, growing into the formidable four-chambered organ that serves the entire body. The heartbeat, that mysterious evidence of aliveness, begins at about 4 weeks but is brought into awareness by the mother at about 16 weeks. This is the quickening spoken of in so many religious texts. And, I often ponder on this great mystery for any man, imagining a new life with its own heartbeat growing inside.

I think again, now, at age 65 about the shock my parents felt when they were told they were having a child. I wondered whether there had been any joy or rejoicing, and I had once asked Gareth this question, if they were happy to have not just one child but two, all at once. But he had looked sad and hesitant and said he wasn't sure. He hinted that they were suspicious that all would not be well and so turned more fervently to their prayers. I was always aware of their deeply religious views. Apparently when the pregnancy was confirmed, so late on, so late in my mother's life, she and my father imagined that the child must be a gift from God. Even more so when we turned out to be two. But I wonder now, was their religiosity around us a way of camouflaging being able to accept and relate to us, was it a way of distancing us from the reality of being infants and children who cried, screamed, made a mess and got in the way? I feel an immediate sense of betrayal for having this thought. I can hear my mother's voice: 'How dare you question us!'

There was also the immediate guilt I felt when I saw their bodies after the car accident. I had insisted on being taken to see them before they were buried, even though Gareth tried to stop me. 'You are much too young Max.' But I knew that I wanted to see them for myself so that I would always know and be sure. And I wondered then, had we exhausted them so much that they drove carelessly, dangerously, in such a hurry to get away? Should I have prayed more for their safety? Was it all my fault?

Madness. Taking blame at ten-years-old. Because I had not followed them ardently in their religions, had not believed enough. There it was, my child's learned omnipotent guilt for something I could not possibly be guilty for.

Chapter 9

In one of our earlier sessions, I had asked Agnes the obvious question about boyfriends. She had shaken her head and looked down.

'No definitely not. I'm not interested.'

'Say more,' I had asked. There was a long silence. 'Have there been boyfriends in the past? '

She smiled, and shrugged, 'Of course, not many and they've come and gone, like my mother's I guess.' She pulled the scarf around her hands. I could see shapes of leaves within the web of wool. I was about to ask if they were sexual relationships when she said, 'But there's never been anyone special. No one to whom I mattered.'

Perhaps it was the word special that touched something in both of us. Special. We all want to feel we've been special to someone at some point in life. Someone with whom we may relax deeply and trust with all that we have. Be ourselves in the present moment – body, mind, emotion, spirit – and also have the freedom to grow and evolve. With whom we can get things wrong or be angry and they love us just the same. Not condemn us to stony silences, as did my mother and Agnes'. Someone for whom we do not have to constantly prove our worth; to have to earn love, to always be on alert in case love gets cancelled.

'No one who made me feel as if I mattered.' She said it again, so sadly.

'And now?'

She shuddered. 'Definitely not now.'

I knew that there was more, so much more, in relation to men, but it still did not feel as if it were the right time just then.

I smiled and said, 'There's your friends, Anna and Mark'.

'Of course,' she said immediately. 'They have been so very wonderful, of course. I was only thinking about … men. Not friends.'

'Yes, I understand. But it's reassuring to your sense of yourself to know to whom you've been important. Your students for example, who are beginning to come back now. And all of your friends. I think you have several friends, Agnes. Can you accept that having such good friends whom you've known for some time and done many things together is a sign that who you are as a person does matter to them, they care for you and want to be with you. That you have value. And they have and still want to help support you through these difficult times?'

'Yes. I didn't mean to moan.' The scarf was being twisted round and round again.

'I'm not judging you at all, Agnes. What I've learned so far in our time together is that it's hard for you to take in the goodness you clearly generate with your friendships. And perhaps also to feel your own goodness.' I allowed a pause. 'How did you meet Anna?' She brightened at the mention of Anna.

'We met at music college. She is a violinist and we played together in several concerts. We both loved music and Anna would say, like Carole, that music nourishes our souls. We've travelled together over the years as well.'

'I can see that the friendship is really important.

'Yes, yes.'

'And when she started going out with Mark, before they got engaged, did that change anything?'

'I don't really know what you mean, you aren't suggesting… that I was jealous are you?' she looked horrified. 'Mark is a really lovely man, one of the nicest. And I was genuinely pleased for Anna. He was her first serious boyfriend.' She looked down. 'She's often said that she'd love it if I were able to meet someone I could just relax with, relax and be happy. She and Mark did try and fix me up with someone in the early days. I went along with it, went out as a foursome at first. But I…I just couldn't continue with it…'

I really felt for her at this point.

'I'm guessing that it's intimate relationships that have been really difficult, and painful. And from what you've told me about your mother so far, she's a tough role model.'

She remained silent, looking down.

'Special. As if I mattered.' I mused on these words. They felt important. I wondered if she had ever felt that she mattered. To someone. Mattered enough in order to let go. Let go physically, sexually and emotionally. She was an attractive young woman, just thirty when we first met. Her child had been conceived and born the year she was twenty-eight. I've always considered that time of life to be a transition point, adulthood established and then the dilemma about 'what next?' appears.

After hearing about her mother, I wondered how it must have been to grow up not knowing who your father was and with a mother who had had many different boyfriends, who came and went in the night. What effect might that have had on her attitude to love and bonding, to sexuality, and to being a woman living in a female body?

I wondered if she had rejected her own sexuality, perhaps feeling repulsed by her mother's behaviour, caught up in the paradox of overt sexuality and denial. The scenes and noises she must have witnessed over the years. I wondered also if her mother had made her take part in some of these sexual practices. I wondered if it was one of her mother's casual boyfriends who had assaulted and raped her, made her pregnant which was why she had repressed any memory so fiercely. But those were just thoughts, analyses. They didn't ring true with what I felt with Agnes in the room. There was something so painfully pressurised and shamed. There was something important and mysterious about that weekend with friends in Cracow and what might have happened there after their visit to Auschwitz–Birkenau. I did also think of Agnes being exposed to such graphic evidence of pain and desperation illustrated in all those photographs; the haunting of thousands of lost souls, and the lost souls in Agnes ancestry. Had she connected with something to do with all of them in a wordless way? It must have been very soon after that visit that her child was conceived. March, the premature birth in late October. It was through her body that some new life was trying to emerge, and to land. The image of the lost child inside her was profound, and I pondered on the idea that her unconscious might have been trying to bring something of the life that had been condemned into conscious awareness, and which had previously been impossible. I didn't know where I was going with these thoughts but there was something about birth, death, fear and the place of understanding and love that I too was trying to fathom in myself.

I also thought more about fear. The vast feelings of fear in Germany, Poland and the camps, collective fear. When does fear become bullying? Can we be bullied by fear and allow it to bully others? Was this something her mother had inherited?

In those early years I kept holding onto an idea that more memories might emerge in alignment with the time of years. The date in late October, when her child was born. I wondered if the timing of this event was stored in her body memory and if so where it might be, and how could we access it. She was so at one with the Spring and her joy in the detail of new life involved in Spring was evident. I wondered if in the autumn the colours of the trees, the fading light, the call of the owl, might also carry memory. But I also knew that these memories, if that was the right word for them, and of an event so profound might never be realised. It felt as it was probably too early to mention it and she would simply panic at the idea and there would be no possibility of an embodied response. But I let the thoughts linger and develop within me as they needed.

It was in the January of our fourth year together and I was playing Shostakovich, the beginning of the Violin Concerto, on the morning of her regular session and she once again arrived early. Carole was with her. They entered quietly, both listening to the complex sounds of the violin. Agnes was moving her hands up and down her body. Carole stood, composed, watching. I turned the music off.

'A new year's gift, doctor,' she said her eyes shining. 'And for me. I want to show you something,' she said.

She knelt on the floor and moved into what I knew to be the Child Pose in yoga. 'Please, join me,' she asked, signalling for me to take a place on the mat beside her.

I did, creaking somewhat around the knees. Carole watched. It was interesting, especially after my experiences of tracing the development of the heart. This time I was on my knees and then bending forward, my arms behind. Then on all fours, stretching my back firstly in an upturned U shape and then right down, elongated onto my feet. There my head was tucked under on a level with my belly. A foetal position. We remained like this for some time.

She looked across at me, still in the pose. 'The Child Pose,' she said. 'I'm learning it. Learning something of the body position of being a child.' She looked directly at me. 'I was a child in this position once, inside my mother, we all were. I wanted to see what it felt like. And of course, it's the shape of the child that lived inside me.' Her look was challenging.

'If I can begin to understand this, how we are all linked, how our bodies work, then I might understand more. And find a way to understand that a child once lived inside me.' There were tears in her eyes. 'And, of course, I must find a way to understand and accept why I did not know that a life lived inside me, even moving inside.' There were tears in her bright blue eyes at this point. 'Not that I can imagine this. But it's what Carole says. She's had to do some horrible things and more horrible things to shut the other horrible ones out. I have to find a way to accept what happened, and what I.. did... or didn't do...' Carole was looking fondly at her. There was a long, shared silence. I was very moved by these events. 'I'm learning from Carole,' she said, and then added shyly. 'I still go to quigong each week but now Carole is teaching me some yoga. She says it helps us all become more aware of our bodies. And that you helped her learn about the language of the body. It's what she got from you, Doctor.'

I was intrigued.

She said again: 'That child pose is what the child inside me was like. Carole has been encouraging me to imagine it.'

It was the first time she had mentioned that the child once lived inside her, and she had done so twice.

After they had gone, I sat outside watching the wren lifting its tiny tail on and off the leaves of the sycamore. My notes from my morning reading read: When we can step back and see everything, that's when we start experiencing realisation and enlightenment. We see the nature of everything because we have the flexibility and the adaptability; we can spread out.

I was spending more time at the cottage in Suffolk. Despite, or perhaps because of, all the memories, I had kept it since Margaret's death in the waves close by, and my parents' deaths on those Suffolk roads. Over time it had become a place of retreat, a place for reflection, for gathering some of the threads of my life. My early morning and evening walks along the beach, so often deserted, brought new friends, terns, the avocets who had made their home at Minsmere, sand martins. And the ocean herself, the variety of waves sweeping the pebble beach or dragging on the thin spit of sand. The music of the waves, reminding me of the opening chords from Britten's Peter Grimes. The orchestral waves, rising and falling, full of life, sometimes exquisite, sometimes menacing. I would often hear the haunting sound of the violins from Dawn. I wondered about a new dawn, for me in my life moving deeper into my sixties, and Agnes, would she find a new dawn in her third year with me?

As time went on, I seemed to be drawn to Suffolk more and more and went most weekends. I was called by the wind over the waves, the smell of the salt marshes and the sea. In summertime the sea lavender bloomed over the heath in a warm lavender carpet, and I would walk within it breathing in the fragrance. But now, early in the year I embraced the harshness of the wind and set out in the early morning feeling light on my feet like never before. Perhaps this was the dancer in me I had never experimented with, and then I laughed at my vanity. But Agnes too, she had shown me the dancer in herself and invited me to join. And I had, safely after all. No reprisals. 'Look you,' I said to my mind, 'just stop it...' I looked across the pebbled beach, Southwold to my left, Sizewell power station to my right. Two extremes, two emblems of difference and change.

Perhaps it was time for me to leave London altogether? To leave work and spend more time here, get involved in local affairs, take up bird watching, walk more... and do what, thinks my morally correct self. And be lonely says another voice, probably from my heart.

I walked on the beach in the very early morning, sometimes as the light of day was only just beginning and I would watch as the sun gradually rose over the sea, the silhouette of boats across its glow.

When the tide was full, and the beach covered in pebbles I walked in strong shoes. At low tide, my favourite, I could walk in the water with my bare feet touching the grainy sand, rejoicing in the caress of sea water no matter how cold. I'd walk, watching and feeling the water pouring over them; at times standing to take deep breaths and to smell the salt from the waves. I worked out from the tides when the best stretch of sand would appear so that I could walk often in bare feet bringing my feet in touch with sand and sea water. Over and over again, I bent down and embraced the water, splashing it onto my face, tasting the salt, raising my face to the early morning sky and the flying terns and sand martins. I had a sense of existential bliss as I embraced each moment. Timeless, faultless, perfect.

One morning a young puppy rushed up to me and began playing, inviting me more deeply into the waves, her deep brown eyes appealing, teasing, inviting me in. So, I joined her and we rolled together spontaneously, both of us like young puppies, laughing, playing, crying with laughter.... Laughter , the great medicine!

I could not at first see the puppy's owner, but then a young, so I thought, woman in jeans and sweater rushed down from the cliffs calling to her puppy, looking concerned, embarrassed.

'Lo siento, perdon...' she said leaning down to try to put her excited puppy on its lead.

I was fascinated, happy.

'Please, no worries' I said. 'I am enjoying it very much, feeling puppyish myself.' She stood still and laughed.

'You are wet through,' she said, then pulled me up as my feet dug further into the sand and I almost fell into her, both of us laughing.

'You speak English as well as Spanish...'

'Claro... and you... you ... enitendes...' She laughed a wonderful light laugh. Then she said, in extremely good English: 'What a way to meet.'

'A lovely way.' I said smiling and, we walked together along the beach, her hairy Labradoodle puppy rushing in and out of the shallow waves. I did not feel cold at all, I felt warm and joyous. I felt totally in that moment, just as I was. Wet, sixty-odd, happy, excited.

To our right was the Dunwich cliff which had begun eroding in the 13th and 14th centuries due to huge storms at sea. Over time the gradual erosion took with it the great city of Dunwich with its famous port, all its houses, Medieval churches and spiritual communities.

'A holy place there was once,' she said waving her hand to the right and bowing. I just loved her voice and her Spanish accent. And I was immediately intrigued by her, wanted to know more, and more. I turned to her, looking into her face.

'I do love it here,' I said.

'I can tell,' she said laughing.

'I've not seen you here before on the beach…are you local?' I asked.

'I just came, from Barcelona.' She looked suddenly serious.

'I read about this place, the city under the sea, yes? a place of magic I think… yes?'

I smiled. 'Certainly,' I confirmed.

'I've rented a place for a few months, translating a book about coastal life, birds.'

'Are you indeed…I shall have to find out more'.

She laughed, running ahead with her puppy. I didn't want her to go. But by then I was getting cold from the sea water.

'I've got a cottage near here… let's turn back now and walk there. It's been in my family for generations. So, come in and I'll make us some tea… get some dry clothes on too…'

She stood coyly, those wonderful blue eyes looking straight into me.

'Ah, you… what do they say... pick me up, sir?'

I knew then that I wanted her. I just wanted her. All inhibitions swept away. I could hardly contain myself, wanting to grab her and go back into the water and thrash around with her in the waves in ecstasy until we were both exhausted…

'What's your name?'

She laughed, 'Call me Fran' she said, and a bolt of lightning went through me.

Chapter 10

Fran! Short for Francisca. She was a forty-something Spanish writer spending several months on the Suffolk coast bringing up to date and translating an old large, illustrated book about certain historic areas on the coastline of Britain. Her commission would also take her to Wales and Scotland so she would be moving on within possibly a couple of months to Wales. No. Those are the events which brought her here to the UK and to Suffolk. Chance? Good fortune? Whatever had brought her here she was a luscious, delicious, active, intelligent and creative person who had stepped into my life from the waves, just like that.

I felt like an adolescent again, as if now, at last, I was able and ready to continue my adolescent explorations. And in my sixties, never too late! The invitation was to feel fully alive in the union with another.

I was thrilled, transported, taken over. She knew exactly how to be with me and what to concentrate on. She was an exuberant Spaniard, single and happy to remain that way. She wanted no commitment which gave us both a curious freedom and challenged my over-responsible habits intensely.

'Tener libertad, libertad… Be free, Dotore Maxwell, be free. My name means free,' she told me, laughing. 'And I intend to live it to the full!'

I went to Suffolk every weekend, extending my weekend to include Fridays and sometimes returning to London Monday morning early.

In March that year Agnes left a message cancelling her next appointment because she'd 'had a memory' and she could not speak of it. I called her back and encouraged her to come, perhaps with Carole. But she did not reply. This had happened before, and I was both concerned and intrigued. I wondered what the memory could be and hoped that she would find the courage to return. It took her a month, and she returned in early April when the glorious magnolia was in full bloom and the many coloured croci had lifted their heads and opened, the bluebells were in bud. Agnes looked serious, older in some ways. She came alone except for her companion scarf.

'No music today, doctor' she said solemnly. 'And that's

as it should be, for there's no music to go with this memory.' She took a large breath, her hand on her solar plexus. 'It was the smell. Smell. A man, well dressed for a visit to us at the clinic, collar and tie, formal shoes. He arrived, and I smelled it immediately. I've not smelled it since. Aftershave. Eternity of all things. Calvin Klein'. She collapsed back into the chair. 'Eternity. That's what I learned it was called. What a name, did they expect it to last for ever?'

She held my gaze. She was silent for some time. I waited in anticipation.

'That last night in Cracow.' She looked at me expectantly. 'So, I'll have to plunge in, if I can. I have made notes from the memories that kept arriving after that smell at the clinic.' She wrinkled her nose. 'A memory – I presume it is that, yes it must be. Perhaps what you would describe as a body memory, the senses leading the way.' She was stumbling.

'Agnes, just go slowly, slowly read to me a line of your memory as you've written it down.',

'Yes, yes…I'm stalling, I know. It's all pretty horrible. That day. Auschwitz Berkenau, that awful day full of horrors. I've not been able to look at any proper information about it since.' Do you mind if I walk around?'

'No of course not, please take your time and move as you need to.'

She stood, the scarf loosely around her, her hands making movements around each other.

'As you know from Anna, we went to church and lit candles. We prayed for those lost souls, we tried to offer something of what Bernie Glassman had offered with his group. Hope, love, bearing witness. But I just couldn't, I think that my mind was too filled with horror. Those images, all the hair that's been kept, the photos; the faces, children in line, over a million and a half children…'

Her voice was choking. She looked at me and I saw the intense grief in her face.

'And then somehow, associations from my own history. And my mother's history. I was looking at the hair, the objects taken from Jewish people and kept thinking of my grandparents, what they had suffered and countless others some of whom might well have been related to me, distantly. So much has been lost. Just lost. Cruelly wiped out. And we now, survivors I suppose are left with these images, facts. What might they tell us, what might we learn...'

I felt so moved, so very very moved at how she was speaking, at how brave she was.

'And... and... God, the babies, dead babies... I saw them and then of course... mine too... am I haunted?' she looked at me with desperate eyes.

'You are not haunted Agnes,' I said firmly. 'But you are having to find a way to make conscious so much of your ancestry and that can feel like a haunting. Many people do use that word to describe what feels like ghosts from the past...'

'But then, how can something like that remain buried?'

I could feel her helplessness. We shared the intense silence.

'And' she continued,' where, how does all that live on inside the survivors... in my mother, is it in me... does it remain somewhere. Do we carry the seeds of our ancestors and their suffering?'

'It can feel as if we do.'

She shrugged, looking lost.

'And I feel as if, when we do become aware, we must make amends, do something...'

She said it with such passion, I had not seen this so fully in her before.

'So,' she looked up, 'I must get to the point, I know. After the church we found a café in the square and sat together mostly in silence. We were all stunned. I don't think any of us could eat much. We probably drank too much wine trying to settle our nerves.' She paused, then said quietly, 'the nerves on fire after Auschwitz,' she nearly choked on the word. 'Then a man came across from one of the other tables and asked if he could join us. Smartly dressed, collar and tie, an American, charming. I've just realised, like the smartly dressed man in the clinic... God... more associations... what we see, what we hear, what we smell... all the senses, yes, you've spoken of them haven't you. Of course. But this man in the restaurant, I'd not noticed him before. We probably all felt we didn't want anyone interrupting, but of course', she laughed harshly, 'we were typically British, polite! So, we invited him to sit with us and shared a drink and he raised a glass to "You British."' She looked desperately sad. 'Then he said, and I do remember this clearly, he had a soft voice, a soft American accent: 'I feel for you British in this place, and your links with Europe. Facing it all must be so very very hard. Is that right?'

We shared a few moments of silence together.

'He must have overheard some of our conversation. Anna and Mark trying to console me, trying to comfort me. All of us shocked. We didn't say much, we were hardly in the mood for conversation. But he tried to be friendly. I do remember that, so I suppose I was drawn in.

And I drank far too much,' she said, really quietly. 'I don't remember of course, but I guess I must have.'

She took a large gulp of water.

'Dancing started in the square. This man, I don't even recall his name. He invited me oh so, so politely and charmingly to dance and I just stood up and seemed to immediately fall into him. I can't believe I did this now.'

Tears poured down her face.

'What on earth was I thinking. But Anna and Mark, they had smiles, they were glad I think because here was some sort of distraction, even an unexpected comfort. What Anna calls the comfort of strangers. Like the film, "The kindness of Strangers" film set in Berlin. She paused before saying, 'she has a point I know intellectually. But, but...'

She took another large drink of water before continuing.

'My main memory now is of waking the next morning, late, in a strange bedroom in our hotel. Eternity on the sheets. Eternity, everywhere.' There was a long pause. 'No sign of the man. I think his name might have been Mark. I felt sick. I was sick. '

She stopped, looking so wretched, leaning forward as if about to throw up.

'We can have a pause,' I said slowly. 'Let's just pause. Lean back and take some breaths.'

We practised some slow breaths together. Her shoulders came down a little.

'Now. Your eyes are closed, and I wonder what you see Agnes.' She was silent. Tears rolled down her face. 'Are there any images of that night, just allow anything to rise however random.' Silence. 'Can you remember what you were wearing that night.'

She coughed and leant forward and again I wondered if she might be sick.

'Slowly.'

She shook her head.

'I was too ashamed to go down to breakfast and face Anna and Mark. We were leaving that day. I didn't know how I was going to get through it. I went to my own room and put the clothes in the bin.' She had folded the scarf around her head and was burrowing in it and I knew that we would have to return to this time.

'Have you told any of this to Anna?'

'No of course not. I've only just remembered it. It's so, so horrible.' There was another long pause. 'When I got home, I burned the rest of my clothes. I had to go to the school where I teach and ask to put things on their fire. The man who looked after the playing field was kind and luckily not curious. I burned all underclothes.' she whispered. 'I know now, I burned them. What remains is only the smell, the smell of Eternity.'

We shared another long silence.

'I've tried, this last month to remember more. I've tried, tried with my body as you, and Carole have suggested, doing my yoga and Chi qong. It's as if my mind, my thinking mind, just does not want to go there.' She stood up and began pacing slowly around the room. 'But I have noticed this; perhaps when I'm not trying too hard, I notice new things. My body moves mysteriously, all of its own, in a sort of dance, a dance of possible pleasure. Something I've not known.' She looked down, suddenly even more shy. 'Forgive me but there are even snippets, snippets of some kind of intertwining of the two bodies, two very different bodies.' She looked at me shyly. 'But it's vague and I wonder whether I've made it up. Obviously, I had sex with him, didn't I, a complete stranger, unheard of. So, somewhere there must be a memory – is that right?' She breathed heavily. 'Once or twice listening to Swan Lake of all things, I've been startled, shocked, by a twinge, probably in my pelvic area, sorry doctor, and, I can't believe I am saying this but something actually potentially delightful, pleasurable so, beautiful I guess if it were... I don't know, not so forbidden, if it hadn't been so awful. At least that what my mind is telling me. How could I do that, of all things, go off with a man I'd only just met after a day of horrors and stay all night in his bed?'

I felt for her deeply and some of what she was saying took me straight back to my time with Frances. Forbidden guilty pleasure. And I knew the difference between forbidden pleasure and the freedom of allowing one's body to lead the way into shared pleasure on so many levels. But I marvelled at these memories that I could imagine so well. Those forbidden fields of gold in Oxford and now, in this room, the image of a possible field of gold one evening in Cracow. That entering, that glorious coupling of two bodies simply lost in pleasure, each other's, their own. Glorious. Fields of gold to be burned and flattened by the consequences of daring to enter. Fields of gold never entered again. That had to be paid for by abstinence and service. So much repressed loss and heartache, so much destruction and death.

Why? How had this potentially glorious realm of the body, the body leading its natural way, following its appetites, basic body pleasures of entering and receiving been touched into and immediately become forbidden, for both of us, Agnes and myself. What kind of learning moved in so quickly. I really felt for her. I reached forward:

'Agnes, what you have remembered is really fantastic, well done to you. It's an important start. This may have been the moment of your child's conception.'

She winced. 'God, oh God.'

I asked her to keep a journal of all the memories, particularly body memories that were arising. I suggested that Carole might help, and she looked away.

'I can't tell Carole any of this.'

I was quiet.

She shrugged. 'Well, it's so shameful isn't it. Carole is my friend; I don't want her thinking awful thoughts.'

'You could keep an open mind and see what arises when

you are with Carole. When do you see her?'

'Well, I've not seen her much lately. I think she's got a pash on someone, another woman. She looks very starry eyed. She's OK at the clinic etc and we did go to a concert together last month. But...'

I waited. 'But?'

'It's not the same. Not as it was. She doesn't seem so interested. I don't blame her at all. She probably has guessed that something unthinkable happened. And I don't want to be a bore.'

I wanted to repeat the word 'unthinkable,' but it felt too soon. I understood it might be how she would react only too well. The paradox of what probably felt like guilty pleasure in the face of death. Guilty pleasure that had to be banished before it could find a place in life. And of course, I could resonate with that.

'Anna?'

'I think Anna guesses something big happened that night. But she is so discreet. She's just waiting for me to open up I think.'

'Sounds like a real friend.' She smiled then. It was truly beautiful. 'Perhaps you could look at Anna's photos again for that would show more of how you looked that night, what you were wearing. You might also see the American man somewhere in the distance. It might help us reconstruct that evening and night and begin to put some of the jigsaw pieces together.'

She shuddered to begin with. 'Ok 'she said slowly.

After she had gone, I was pleased that I had time to reflect on this last session. I was full of a mixture of feelings and thoughts. Really happy that this memory had emerged and that she was brave enough to speak of it. I was also fascinated by the fact that both Agnes and I had secrets of this nature to hide. Forbidden pleasure to be immediately banned. Now that this was named and indeed shared it became a living experience for us to explore. Agnes would of course never know of my own experience, but I did wonder whether something of the energy I was now daring to explore might help her own awakening. My own memories, past and present, flooded in, took over. I played piano, Beethoven moonlight sonata...so often hackneyed and played for sentimentality. But I loved its slow beginning, it's heartbeat of familiarity, its beauty, before the crescendo. I imagined the conception of new life, the embryo of a human child. The child who might have been brought into life for Agnes. A child that might have been mine to love and cherish. But ours were children not destined to live. And why. Why could they not live?

Were we so awful, unfit. I knew this was completely illogical but there was such a feeling of badness, yes badness, being bad, that emerged from that session. I felt it in Agnes, and I felt it in myself. Beethoven, The questioning notes, the rhythm, repetition, questions over and over. Conception. Such a magnificent but hidden gift inside the body. Two people coming together to make three. The quickening of Beethoven's notes, the speed, the rush as there is at the sexual climax. That glorious spaciousness within togetherness where we forget our mortality, where there is only the bliss of now, of the moment, of not wanting it ever to end.

How I had lost myself in Frances. I had wished I had been able to continue with more encounters instead of branding them dangerous, forbidden and to be banished. But now I had found myself in the arms of another beauty. Fran, gorgeous Fran, and the life and energy between us so unexpected, spontaneous and completely utterly allowed. I'd allowed my body to open up enough to lead the way.

And Agnes, how understandable that she had responded to the invitation to lose herself after the trauma of witnessing recordings of the horrors that had penetrated her ancestors, which her mother still carried in her silence of hatred.

Chapter 11

Eternity. What a name! The power of fragrance to release memory haunted me.

Memories of my times with Frances in Oxford appeared in many forms. I tried to remember the perfume she wore. I never knew what it was, I had no interest in the names of perfumes in those years. The gifts I took her were ones I imagined were romantic – flowers gathered from the meadows off St John's and poems I had written. She had laughed, apparently delighted so I thought then, and flung her arms and legs around me pulling me happily onto whatever surface was available. That perfume, rich and earthy, possibly sandalwood and lavender of some kind, seemed to be in accord with our sensual and sexual adventures. It became an extension of her, not something I might look for in a bottle. How I had revelled and rolled in that fragrance, sucked and savoured it. Just these sense memories made my body tremble, my loins come alive. If I had come across the actual smell of her since that time perhaps more memories could have surfaced for me and put me more in touch with body memory. Maybe it had already, and I had banished it immediately. How powerful are our early imbedded learnings of control. I felt anguished when I thought what that smell memory might have offered me. Would it have helped me to take more risks perhaps, to engage more with women, to let my body lead the way into sensual and sexual experiences? Or would it have awakened my 'bad boy' sense, and despair. But there I was again, just thinking about it all, analysing, not getting on with just living it, as Philip would say.

But I knew from my years of work that openings in memory come when they have opportunity or are ripe and ready, which is when it feels safe enough. You cannot prise them out, especially when they are related to past trauma. I still ponder on the multitude of meanings of safety, how individual this is. 'Play for safety' one of my house matrons used to say, a frightened woman fearing danger in every simple corner, seemingly unsuited to work in a boys' school. And if I had searched for the fragrance?

But those nights all came back once Agnes had shared

her time in Cracow. Those nights, the days, the movements, the sighs, Sting and fields of gold ... all of it.

And now, how could I be now, at the same time as almost reliving those earlier days.

Fran wore little fragrance but to me she smelled always fresh, wonderful, her skin so soft and glowing. She seemed to have the radiance of Spring freshness. I laughed at myself, at my boyishness. Being in love put a rosy glow over everything. But wasn't I so lucky, so late in life. Fran had gone to Wales to check out accommodation but was coming back to Suffolk in ten days. I was determined to find out what perfume she enjoyed, probably childish of me but I so wanted that memory. Just in case. When I stood back a little my therapist self thought that probably Fran's absence was a useful space after the session with Agnes. I needed to make use of the time to clear some of my own regressed memories and return to the present. But I did feel somewhat regressed! And how I missed her and everything she was, all we did together! A heartache.

I went to Suffolk alone and walked along the beach, the sound of the waves teasing me now. Taunting...a thin echo calling me in the sound and rhythm of the waves, in and out, in and out, and I could only think of what else goes in and out ... Up and down ... that takes us beyond our ordinary selves into some other universe. Often on those lonely mornings I just wanted to crash into the waves and roll around just like I had on the morning I met Fran. And all those times ... those earlier wonderful times that I had banished from memory of any kind. It seemed to me that all those years ago in Oxford I responded instinctively to play, to dance and kiss, to rub my body over another, to be aroused and seek release and sexual satisfaction. And now I was having to learn to take the risk of finding all this again in a different way. All this that Fran was handing me on a plate! But it also brought me into vital physical contact with my past. My fears.

I did feel in moments as if I was being released from the great hand of control I had experienced throughout my early life; in school, in feeling responsible for Margaret, in not being magically good enough to save her or my parents from their early deaths. Those moments in Oxford with Frances gave me spaces where I simply let go. For the first time. She wanted me, just as I was, her embrace and desire were unconditional, she showed me something of freedom. I had my twenty-first celebrating with her, in secret. I was just starting out into adult life, a time when those used to being with more forms of freedom perhaps can experiment on all levels, explore more and more, gain independence and strength. But I was already too restricted by fear of judgement, too hobbled internally and externally to experiment with youth. I never did feel young. Oxford offered so many opportunities, but it was only within the secret forbidden world with Frances that I was able to drink in like a thirsty animal. I had no living relatives, for even Gareth had died by then. I had no close friends; I was lonely and isolated. Frances' warmth and invitations were so utterly welcome. I drank them in.

But, but, at the first stumbling block to adult maturity I had shut down. I was like Agnes, shutting down after the horror and shame of responsibility for an unknown dead child.

All those years later, Agnes awakened these memories, and I visited them afresh.

I began looking for the kind of books I was reading then – Brave New World, the poetry of Eliot and Yeats. 'The Second Coming' was always a favourite. And for Philip too ... those words ...we shared them often: 'What rough beast ... slouches towards Bethlehem to be born?' And now I was startled by Yeats' words all over again, and excited to find out more about the rough beast in myself, in everyone.

The music Frances and I listened to, the extremes. Marianne Faithful, Wagner, and of course Sting when he was with The Police. 'Hungry for you' we sang together in French, leaning closer and closer together. Years before 'Fields of Gold', which I only discovered much later. But that unique voice, which can get under the skin and into the heart, was still there. This was an opening. I had a new freedom of a kind.

I kicked stones along the beach and bent to collect them to throw into the waves. My body felt great surges of anger and despair that rose with heat from my stomach and what I imagined as rage stuck in my throat. Anger with myself for my cowardice, my preciousness, believing I could hide away.

My body was right in it all, I wanted to kick, spit, shout, repeat obscenities I had heard but never used. How could I have been so neglectful of all that I knew. But only in my head. You fool Max, You stupid stupid fool.

Stuffed shirt, Emily had called me; 'Mr Perfect you think you are ... well you don't fool me.' What had she seen, if anything, when she had stopped seeing me as her rescuer from a life in an institution? What had I done to myself by marrying Emily? It felt that I had allowed her to suck out my life force and energy by choosing the role of rescuer. And I had continued to do this to myself on many levels.

As ever, Philip was there, with his Aussie brogue which he never lost, and which lent real timbre to his words, whilst I was standing in the waves one morning. It was as if he grabbed me by the shoulders and shook me: 'Yes, yes, you be angry, just let it out. All that fire and brimstone in your belly. Years of it! You need to kick and shout; you need to properly lament.' I had a vision of him. His eyes were clear blue and filled as he was speaking. Mine too, and I was choked.

I fell onto my knees, bending my head in the water allowing the salt of both tears and waves to wash over, to sting me awake, to have their way. The mighty sea with its rhythms of in and out ... the rhythms of the sexual and sensual embraces I had briefly known, so early on and then lost. In, out, harsh, gentle, moving in and out. I did this over and over, relishing it all.

And now, right now in my life, images of Fran, fully present, alive, her smile, laugh, invitations to me arose from the waves. I would continue to enjoy being with her every minute. I felt lucky, so very lucky and I stood in the sea with my heart bursting, tears pouring down my face to join the waves in simple gratitude.

After the revelation of the night in Cracow the energy between Agnes and I seemed to change. It became almost conspiratorial, and I feared that the intimate sharing might lead us to become too involved in ways I had no control over. This was as close to my own issues than anyone else I had ever worked with. And it was all about sex – forbidden sex – and what arose from it. No doubt there would be moments of frisson which at first, I felt I would fear. But I learned to be less afraid as we went along. I also knew that the fact of the sharing, and my being so affected by it and so aware of our similarities, was important. We were both uptight people full of guilt who had spent our whole life so far trying to be good and work hard to stave off some form of guilt for the past. Guilt that was not ours, not our responsibility. I had to maintain a professional self and put myself fully into our work together and take more risks at the same time.

Now we had a likely conception date we went very slowly trying to piece together the months of her pregnancy. Again, I found myself thinking in the shower of the heart and the heartbeat. The heartbeat of an unborn child, new life in potential. We were moving close to the months when Agnes, had she been aware of being pregnant, might have noticed her child's heartbeat.

Perhaps it was a bit abstract, but I began speaking of it to Agnes after I had listened to Philip Glass' Violin Concerto, particularly the third movement, which always filled me with feeling and awareness of the heart. I suggested we find words or music that would echo a heartbeat wherever it was ... the heartbeat of the world, each individual living being, the heartbeat of the earth herself. In so doing I hoped we might be able to share a sense of interbeing with the many forms of heartbeat that can take place, and feel a connection without judgement. As I reflect on this all these years later, I smile at how idealistic I was, and Agnes also. But because music had brought about such a deep sharing and Agnes was attempting to embrace body movement and energy with her yoga and Tai chi it seemed to work. We both searched for music that resonated with heartbeat. I still felt that finding a heartbeat and moving in time to it would be important. It seemed that this was what all life depended on. Agnes found several pieces called 'Water Dances' which contained the repetition of the same eight notes beloved of Philip Glass, whom both of us enjoyed. She was now keeping a journal daily and writing down any snippets that could be of interest, however odd or different from the subject it appeared.

I listened over and over to that third movement of Glass' Violin Concerto and was continually moved to tears. What possibility, what joy, what continuation. Those eight beats over and over touching on my own heart and heartbeat. The rising to the crescendo, over and over pointing to hope and to union. We sat together and shared again some of what I had I remembered from my reading, that the embryonic heart, travels from the top of the head into the centre of the chest and begins to beat as early as 4 weeks. It becomes more discernible to the mother at between 16 and 18 weeks although this was different for everyone. She held her hand to her belly as we spoke of this and there were times when she tried to imagine it, a heart beating in her child inside her.

'It is a miracle' she said one morning. 'A miracle it happens like this. And so sad, so sad that I never knew.' Her voice dropped. 'I would like to have known.'
We shared this tender moment of her connection.

One day when speaking of her early life she told me how she had begun to watch the ants that crawled over her bathroom floor and was careful with them, setting them free from any splashed water when she washed. She spoke of the ants with such reverence and the silence we shared was contemplative, with a sense of wonder and reverence for life. I wondered if she might have some association with the fragility of her child in utero, but she said sadly, 'My mother stamps on them, shouting, or sprays them.' Then she turned to me, 'We were all like little ants once weren't we? Our life in the womb begins with a tiny ant-like shape.'

I was impressed with her image.

'I feel that being with the ants could teach me something about being small and surviving.' Then she added, 'But too late for my child, my daughter.'

She was saying those words more and more now, claiming her experience.

One of the many themes she spoke of was her continued awareness of nature and her pleasure in it – all the animate life around her favourite pond. The way she followed the mallard ducklings again and listened to their calls. They had been joined by shelduck, a rare find in London. And one day she had seen a kingfisher diving. She commented about the bird's fragility, looking left to right, diving so swiftly into the water and up again, taking flight immediately. And being so very beautiful. It felt as if this new life and its wonders offered by nature around her was becoming a form of awakening. Awakening to what had been silenced within her.

She and Anna were working on creating a musical evening to raise money for refugees who were also invited to join in at any time. Agnes was on piano, Anna on violin, their friends Martin on cello and viola. We had all been reading more and more about refugees making the dangerous Channel crossing to the Kent coast, coming from Afghanistan and from war-torn countries in Africa and the Middle East. 'It's for people trying to find a safe haven,' she said one day, her eyes shining. 'Like I am here.'

Carole's relationship had ended, and she was back spending time with Agnes, and apparently now fully engaged with helping her to find the jigsaw pieces that might restore memory of this time 3 years ago. Carole's approach was much more physical and there were times, when they came to sessions together, that I could see that Carole was on a journey of her own. She was becoming more and more fascinated by the details of women's bodies, not surprisingly I imagined, for now she owned such a body. She wanted to discuss periods and I noticed Agnes squirm.

'But no, Aggie, I want to know, I want to know what it's like to have nothing between your legs so that these fluids can come out. I'll never have that. So, tell me.'

Agnes tried, blushing, and I found myself wading in with practical questions such as what she had noticed about her periods in the months following Cracow. She became thoughtful and Carole looked at me resentfully. Her mouth pouted a little, suggesting I was spoiling the scene.

Later that month Agnes came looking larger in her stomach and stood in front of me proudly announcing that it was Carole's idea to put padding on her in the hope that it might help the memory of carrying the child. She was proud at first but when she sat down tears came easily.

'But, but what if I can't manage these memories she said. Isn't this why I possibly blanked everything out. For to become pregnant … I can only just say the word … pregnant.

And from... from... you know... God... a one-night stand with a stranger. My God... it all seems so careless, heartless, forbidden, horrible. All this, all this is what I have to face isn't it? There's no music for this is there?'

Chapter 12

These, new to me, daily revelations seemed to herald a new focus on my explorations with Agnes. I imagined her returning from Cracow to continue her uncomfortable camping at her mother's house, carrying all those complex and haunting experiences as well as the hidden memory of the night with the American. I asked her if she could reflect back to that time and try to describe her days following that weekend away. She was often silent, or sullen after these questions. At first, she was reticent to speak, looking down at her hands and moving them around inside her scarf.

'It was March - am I right?' I asked.

She gave a big sigh as if reluctant to begin but then nodded. 'Yes, the very beginning of spring; the tiny coal tits were on the feeder.' She looked thoughtful and then looked up at me. 'That Christmas when I had to move in, I bought the feeder as a gift for my Mum. Her flat has a very small balcony and there is a wonderful maple tree outside that belongs to the ground floor flat that has a garden. The coal tits love it.' She sighed again and paused. 'I was trying to express my thanks, that she had…taken me in…but she just sniffed. Then later I did notice her watching and her face looked as if she enjoyed it. But of course, she would never admit that to me …'

The emptiness of the atmosphere around her mother entered the room.

'Do you know why she is like this?'

Agnes just looked down.

'I guess it's her past… I know I've mentioned it before… but I don't know. I just know that I've never been able to make any difference.'

I felt deeply sad and thought that it was none of Agnes responsibility to make her mother happy, but I admired her for her efforts.

'I notice that you never refer to your mother's flat as home.'

She sighed. 'No, it was never a home. Not like other places I've known that feel like homes – Anna's, other friends, the person who taught me piano, other teachers from college

...' she became thoughtful. 'And I think, and I've been thinking of this since I started seeing you, I think I am probably most at home when I am playing music.' Her voice took a pensive tone. 'Music is my home. I've not named it as this before ... the sounds, not just instruments but rivers, the wind, the burst of new life in spring, the fragrance in the woods, they all have sounds, the sounds of natural life in its vast variety. This is where I feel at home, and it feels good. At least I've had this.'

We allowed a warm silence to nourish the space around us. I did wonder whether she had ever allowed herself to get angry, angry with her mother, her circumstances. She had coped by getting out as fast as she could. And of course, anger, expressing it with others, had been my own issue.

'Music...It's the land, isn't it? The land, that's where I belong, can be myself.'

'Indeed.' I paused for a moment, considering what I was about to say next. 'The dream you had, Agnes, the dream you told me when we first met. A dream of a child, a being, who wanted to land with you.'

She sobbed immediately, with great gasps of air. 'Yes, yes, yes ...'

'We will help her find her land yet, Agnes,' I said softly, surprising myself. What did I really mean?

We shared a meaningful silence. Both of us reflecting on the land, the earth that held us, the sounds of the music of the land, the trees, birds, and all the fragrances and transformations the earth could offer to the humans who lived upon it.

'It must have been very hard for you returning to live at your mother's ten years after leaving at eighteen, all those years ago when you'd claimed some freedom and a very different life for yourself.'

She gave a deep breath. 'Yes, it really was. I felt like the hopeless kid again, unwelcome. But I was desperate, no one else had any space. I didn't know when I phoned her if she would... and amazingly she did, grudgingly. I wonder why she did take me in...?'

'I'm so sorry, Agnes.'

'Thanks for saying that, it helps, helps me not to feel quite so b–'

I knew that she was going to say 'bad' but she stopped and just shrugged.

'Did you have any space for yourself, for your music?'

She laughed. 'You must be joking! Anna's friend Mary had stored everything I had from the flat for me in her garage.' She looked up, 'Anna and Mark were in New Zealand when all this happened. They'd rented their flat, and as they arrived back earlier than expected they had to stay with Mark's parents until the tenants moved out. They were concerned when we all met up as I was looking, well, bedraggled I guess and tired. And they were horrified when I told them what it had been like... I didn't tell them all of course, just a bit. Their concern for me, their... love... is that the right word?'

She looked up at me. I smiled, thrilled that she had recognised this in her friends and said softly: 'yes, I think so, Agnes.'

She smiled back, relieved. 'Thanks. Yes. Love. It's why the visit to Cracow was arranged and so soon after they returned. They've had to make lots of adjustments since their return. They had a few months living up in Newcastle for Marks work, and of course Anna now has her lovely son. But throughout all of this they've been wonderful friends.'

I nodded.

'When they did eventually get into their London flat in the early autumn, I did stay over in their sitting room every now and then but...I don't like to intrude on a married couple...' She got up and walked around the room, pulling at the scarf. 'There was nowhere else to go other than my mothers... I suppose she felt it was her duty. Maybe she was even triumphant as now I was like her... a refugee... God, what an awful thing to say!' She sat down with her head in her hands. 'I went to my mother's house with just one suitcase. I sat in whatever room was free. I slept in the sitting room. My mother's place has only one bedroom and I would never want to share with her... ' she shivered and then sighed... 'anyway, she had... she had several male visitors. Sometimes if they were, you know, at it, I just had to sit in the bathroom.' She smiled, looking at me through those sad blue eyes. 'Pathetic isn't it, all that I hoped for, for myself, studying music and trying for an independent life and I end up actually enjoying staring at the toilet bowl as I sat on the side of the bath as it was the safest place to be.'

'Say more, Agnes.'

'It was awful. She has kept the old-fashioned suite, aubergine … an aubergine toilet, sink and bath. And awful tiles with weird objects on them … nauseating.'

'Can you remember anything about how your body felt sitting on the side of the bath?'

'Sick,' she gasped and looked up. Then: 'Of course, I would, wouldn't I?'

I reached over to her wondering. 'So, sitting in the bathroom.'

'Well yes, of course. At least she couldn't see me there. Couldn't see me throwing up, retching …'

I hesitated before asking, 'Did you ever have any inkling of why you were feeling sick, even being sick?'

She gasped. 'Oh god, obvious isn't it,' she sobbed. 'Then, I just thought it was the life, the basicness, the loneliness. Those awful men...' There was a long silence. Then she whispered, 'I've often wondered whether they paid her. She was always short of money. She made so little preparation for later life. Awful isn't it, you're late sixties and you have to do this...'

'Agnes... did any of the men ever try it on with you, or hurt you?'

She wailed.

'I had to be mostly out, out of sight. I guess in case they wanted a younger woman.' She was rubbing her hands together. 'My mother never spoke of it. I never knew when they might be coming so I couldn't plan. But several times I had to run to Anna's friend Mary who had stored my things in her garage. There was no room there, but I could at least sit on their sofa... I felt so, so ashamed...'

She had had to stay at her mother's flat for another 10 months after her weekend in Poland. Every now and then a friend would bail her out for a week or so whenever they had a spare room free.

'When I told my mother I would be moving out for a week or so to give her some space, she just shrugged and folded her arms over her belly. "So, you'll be at someone else's charity then. You want to watch your waistline girl".'

'When exactly did she say this?'

Agnes looked startled. 'It was probably the second time I went to camp at a friend's, probably early August... But there was another reference I'm remembering now, I suppose it was September whilst I was at Mary's. She phoned, actually phoned, and asked me to go round and sort out something to do with the bird feeder. Yes, it was then, it must have been in late August.'

'So you'd be possibly about 4 to 5 months pregnant.'

She looked shocked.

'Do you remember what you wore that day?'

She nodded, 'Yes. I had something new as I was organising a charity concert again.' She looked up. 'I remember feeling, at last I am doing something useful again.' Then, after another thoughtful pause she said, 'Anna and I prepared together, she was going to play something too, and we went shopping for some new clothes for her. She bought the dress for me in the sales... Anna again coming to my rescue, gosh I am so lucky... and of course my mother always noticed when I had something new. She would happily look disapproving and say something about money and 'It's alright for you'. One day she even said, 'You've done well for yourself.'

Agnes' mother was making me feel really uncomfortable, and angry. I was about to speak when she said, 'Oh I see now, of course. Yes, it was a bit tent like, comfortable ...'

'Was your mother the first person to make a comment on you gaining weight?'

She nodded. 'She is obsessed with the body size of women ... well all people really, a real fattist. Even though she's always been very slim, to me anyway, she wears a sort of corset thing, like women in the 1950's used to wear. To give her a shape I think...a shape of a...well I suppose curvy, even sexy woman.' She bent forwards muttering into her scarf... 'God it's hard to speak of one's mother in this way. I feel... disloyal, and shocked at the same time. As if I am only just realising. Horrifying...'

I was alerted to this reality. In my reading I had discovered that some women wore corsets to conceal the fact of their pregnancy. Perhaps her mother had done this when she was carrying Agnes. Perhaps Agnes was an unwanted child from the beginning.

'I wonder if you could either bring that dress to your next session or wear it, noticing how it feels and if any memories or associations arise?'

She came in the dress for her next session. It was pale pink, embroidered at the hem, charming and not particularly maternal. It suited her. Her mother must have been really charged up to accuse her of gaining weight. I wondered what else Agnes' mother had been looking for. I was also aware of possibly jealousy or envy of Agnes' career and way of life. And that fact of Agnes being able to return to it, albeit slowly. It was clear that her mother and their relationship was now entering our work together. It felt as if this was important and the key to a lot of understanding; and that we had a long way to go.

She sat down and said she'd been thinking more about those months with her mother. After our last session the week before, she had visited her mother. 'I'd not seen her since she threw me out after I told her...' Agnes had found her surprisingly compliant. 'I wondered if she might have been actually pleased to see me.'

'Say more.'

'Well, I telephoned first, and she said to come round, no hesitation, no strings, she didn't ask for anything. Surprising.' She looked up at me. 'I do still send a little money when I can ... she worked only as a cleaner and lives on a limited state pension.' She paused. 'She also drinks quite a bit. Anyway, I took flowers, which she always liked. I was friendly and straightforward. I felt, well, I really wanted to try to have a more straightforward conversation with her and not simply seek appeasement. Perhaps my voice was firmer. I even told her that I was having therapy and she raised her eyebrows and shifted in her chair.'

I was so pleased that Agnes had had the courage to mention this. I also wondered if her mother had any tinge of guilt about Agnes and wondered whether she and I spoke about her.

Agnes had tried to tell her mother something of the experience of therapy and how she was trying to remember the events of the time following the Cracow weekend when she had been staying with her, and the events leading to the painful time on Salisbury Plain. Her mother had been sent messages from the hospital following her admission as she was recorded as Agnes' next of kin. She was not told details of what had happened and did not visit. Anna went to see her to find out if she wanted to know more or was worried and offered to take her to the hospital. But she refused, closing down as if she presumed it was something bad and didn't want anything to do with it. Anna had by now expressed her shock at this to Agnes. She had also approached Agnes' mother again when Agnes was at The Maudsley, thinking that it wasn't so far to travel. Apparently Agnes' mother knew that the Maudsley was some sort of psychiatric hospital and her face because even more stony.

'What's she done now?' she asked coldly. Anna was shocked at her cold indifference and never tried to visit again. When she was able to speak of it to Agnes, Agnes nodded and sighed, saying that she thought her mother would be ashamed of her if she knew the details and that Agnes had 'showed her up'.

But now, three years on, Agnes was being firmer. She had been brave enough to tell her mother what had happened, saying to her mother that she realised how ashamed she might feel to be told that Agnes had been pregnant and had given birth to a stillborn babby. And that she, Agnes, had been so deeply shocked by the whole thing that she had absolutely no memory of it and was trying to sort it all out in her mind. She apparently kept saying, 'Please listen to me, for I am so sorry if I cause you distress. But there are some things I do need to know from you, to help me find some release from it. You can help me. Please. There is so much I need to know about you, and about the past.' She said her mother would not look at her, but she had appeared to be listening.

Agnes had persevered. 'What would be really helpful,' she had said, 'would be to know if you noticed anything about me during those months when I was with you and when I was, apparently … pregnant.'

I was so touched by Agnes reporting to me these new conversations with her mother. I felt she was so brave and said so. Agnes smiled at me then. 'I still find the p word, that word so, so difficult.'

At the mention of pregnancy her mother had stood up,

turning away. Agnes had tried to make it easy for her. 'Was there anything you noticed about me during those months?'

'You were getting fat, you were being sick, you stopped drinking coffee, you kept staring out of the window,' said her mother eventually. 'I guess you were on your way ...'

At another session I asked, 'When you got back from the weekend with Anna and Mark, did you tell your mother much about Cracow and visiting Auschwitz Birkenau?'

She swallowed. 'I tried. But she didn't want to know. I knew she felt that way, I knew, but I wanted ... I wanted to ask her about her family, my grandparents and her cousins. I thought, if I appealed to her, one woman to another, she might at least give me something.' Silence. 'She slapped me. "Never mention that place again if you know what's good for you."'

The violence of those words and that time was right in the room, and I felt it physically.

'Let's go back to your recent conversation. It sounds as if you were able to be very different with her this time and that she was able to soften in some way?'

Agnes laughed, 'I don't think she will ever soften. But yes, she was more forthcoming. And I was clearer, more assertive perhaps in a way that wasn't off-putting? I took some of the photographs from the weekend – I will bring them here next time. I tried to reassure her that I now understood something of how painful it all was to think that her relatives had been through this. I asked her if she had any photos. I had asked her before, but I just wondered whether she had some hidden. I am thinking now that she has had some kind of trauma and she is not of the generation to be able to recognise it as such, she just keeps everything under wraps.'

'You are being really brave Agnes; all this is really excellent. You are trying to make connections. Important connections about your family history and trying to understand the suffering there. All this is so important.

'I asked her directly about my birth. I said that I wondered whether she also had become pregnant without realising it until I was on my way. That the fact that I also had been pregnant and not known had brought her own experience back ... And that it all felt impossible for her, and frightening.' Agnes then stood up and moved around the room. 'That was bold of me, wasn't it?'

We sat silently together.

'It was actually, probably, the first tender moment I had had with her, ever. And suddenly I was in control. Amazing. She had tears in her eyes. She said, 'I cannot talk about it. I'm not like your generation wanting to probe into everything... what good does it do?' She actually looked at me properly. I reached for her hands and said, 'Mother, let's go slowly together, exploring as best we can, all that has happened ... and both benefit from my being of my generation and getting help with the painful family history. If I can manage to receive some understanding, even goodness from the process, some release of all that has been hidden, you might also be able to do as well.'

Chapter 13

Soon after the conversation with her mother, Agnes brought up a dream.

'I am captive somewhere, very young, looking out from between slats in a wooden enclosure. It's dark in there and we are pressed up against each other. I see people being dragged away by their hair and their hair cut off; I think it was with shears … imagine … shears … There is screaming. I am shaking. I hide amongst the other children and keep watching for the chink of light in the locked door to become brighter and the door to open. It would be our turn next.'

We sat together in deep silence, both of us shaken by the feeling of the dream. I had to stop my associations going straight to Auschwitz Birkenau and the suffering and murder of her ancestors. As well as its possible family importance, and what she had seen for herself at the camps, the dream also had its symbolic meaning for her personally and for now, and what Agnes was uncovering in the work we were doing. Who or what was holding her captive?

I asked, 'How old do you feel you are in the dream?'

'Really young… Perhaps four.' She gasped. 'I spent Sunday with Anna and her Archie, her son, he's three nearly four now.' She sank into the chair. 'I watched him play with such freedom, running round and round the lawn. He was playing with a couple of colourful windmills … and he and Anna, they are so happy. Mother and son. Happy and free.'

'Do you have your own memories of being that age?'

She shook her head sadly, but her voice took a determined tone.

'But I'm going to ask my mother when I see her next. I feel as if I am on a quest.'

'Let's stay with the feeling of this dream, Agnes. It feels so important that you allow it to become as conscious as possible and find ways to be with it. I am wondering if, when you were little, you had any favourite toys you used to play with, the ones that held bits of magic, like the coloured windmills, or ones that were cuddly, a sort of comforter.'

She laughed and interrupted me. 'Well, I had tiny pink

bear,' she said. 'She was my heroine, she went everywhere with me. I had a big version on my bed and a little pocket one. Pink Bear,' she laughed. 'I haven't thought of her for years.'

'Can you see your pink bear now and feel her in your hand?'

I wondered who might have given this to her and what associations she might have, when she said, 'I think the bears were probably stuffed into a bag of clothes my mother was given, by the woman she worked for ... I will ask her.'

'But these bears were important to you?'

She nodded and touched her heart area. 'They were real gifts ... and for me ...'

'Let us try something Agnes, let us go back into the feeling of the dream for a few moments, we can stop anytime it becomes uncomfortable. And this time you have both pink bears with you as your comforters and witnesses. Is this OK?'

She nodded.

'OK. Put pink bear next to your heart now, Agnes, and hold her gently, and then when you are ready, feel yourself again in that cramped wooden space. Just imagine, feel into it as best you can, if possible, let pink bear help you and stop if you become too frightened. I'm here.'

She closed her eyes, stroking her imaginary bear. Then she sniffed. 'People are out there, I can hear them, they speak in another language. I don't understand it.' She paused, 'it's the smell ... the panels, they had something on them ... oh God, I think it was sweat. But why? Oh God, it's probably fear. The sweat of fear...'

'So, there's the sweat of earlier fear from others and your own fear ... where do you feel it in your body?'

She clutched her abdomen with the hand holding the bear and her throat with another. Then cried out, 'I am going to suffocate; I can never get out.' She cried out and stood up unsteadily, clutching the top of the chair.

I helped her to sit down, and we took three slow breaths together. We then sat with the intense feeling of this dream and the shock. I remember helping her to guide her breathing until it was steady. Then she wept. 'I've not cried like this since ... since it all happened.'

I passed her a pen and paper and suggested she record something of this experience. She drew a small figure at a huge gate and gave it to me with wide eyes. I smiled, receiving it gratefully. When I offered it back to her, she said, 'No, keep it safe for me, Doctor, I don't trust myself with it … not just yet.' Then she stood up and asked me for a hug. She wrapped her arms around me. 'You are such a good man,' she said warmly. 'You really hold me, don't you?' She looked up directly into my eyes. I was surprised. This was a first. I was unsure what I was being told and somewhat nervous of my response. I very rarely hugged patients, especially women, and knew many male colleagues who had got into trouble this way. But since meeting Fran and being able to be aware and trust my own responses, especially physically, and being much more open and trusting of my body, I really felt and allowed the warmth of Agnes' body touching mine. I felt her fragility, sensed her hidden femininity and sensuality. She stroked my back.

Whoops. Where might we be going with this, I thought, two people who had for so long denied the power of touch and of intimacy for fear of its outcome, and for so long in my case.

'Thank you,' she said with sparkling eyes. She picked up the paper with the drawing of the gate and said again, 'keep it here for me, then I know it is safe.'

After she had collected her things, she stood in front of me and said: 'You are quite a man Dr Max Maxwell. I believe you know what men and women are all about.'

I promised to keep the drawing safe and that it would be here for her anytime she was ready to claim it. I said that what she had just shared was fantastic and brave.

After she had gone, I realised I was also flattered and deeply heartened by her finding me 'quite a man'. It felt extraordinarily welcome, and I allowed it in. We were beginning to approach the heart of our journey together.

I thought more deeply about how much early human experience is recorded within the cell memory of our bodies. This can often only find expression in either sensation or words when it is revealed by a conscious or unconscious event. And only then when it is safe enough. I was hopeful that Agnes was beginning to feel safe enough to reveal more of her early history, which I sensed was extremely painful and traumatic. The recent combination of speaking with her mother in a new way, and seeing Anna's son, had triggered this dream with its contrast of imprisonment compared to freedom. As well as this was Agnes' growing awareness of her body's senses, particularly through smell and sound. And now, I could join her as I also became more aware of mine!

I had noticed that when they came to the session together, Carole often stroked Agnes' arm as she was speaking, especially about something painful. And that the touch helped to soften the tension in her face and tightness in her shoulders. It was as if Carole could intuitively sense the intensity of Agnes' feeling or body tension. She had of course made the long complex journey of her own, of recognising her body's calling and making gender transition. This was supported greatly by her learning to listen to all the body's senses, touch, sight, taste, smell, sound; and beginning a useful conversation with each of them. She and Agnes seemed to be getting along well, were affectionate to each other in a way that felt mutual and friendly. I found myself wondering if this shared tenderness could also be sexual, and immediately scolded myself for this thought as if it were directly transmitted from my own life and all that was awakening there. Horror! Thinking about sex between clients! I could see Philip laughing ... and hear his voice ... 'Still thinking that way, Max ... forbidden fruit, eh?' Then 'just get on with it, man, this is life, animation!'

I remembered that when we were working together, Carl, as Carole was then, would often stroke his own arm as he was speaking, particularly about something painful. He wore soft colourful men's clothes that might have been a couple of sizes too big for him, shirts with big patterns and soft colour co-ordinated trousers. A huge change from the figure-fitting army uniform and boots. I asked him once about clothes and what they meant, whether the softness and its touch was important to him, and he had laughed. 'It's Ok here with you, Doctor, as you and I are trying to soften our way out of the hardship of war and what it's left me with. Fat lot of good letting that be known in the army, that I liked the touch of soft colourful clothes,' he said. 'Or in my family of course. Colourful clothes, softness, touch … what, are you a willy woofter or something? they'd have said. I might even have had it beaten out of me.' His eyes were narrowed into bright brown slits. He shrugged and got up and walked around the room before turning to me swaying.

'But yes, when my Mum and sisters were out, I would wait to make sure they really had gone and then go into their drawers and press my face into their soft woollies; glorious. The smell of perfume … violet or a sort of lavender after a birthday or Christmas. The hangers in the cupboards were full of glories, Doc, real glories. I even used to dare to try a dress on every now and then. The feel of it, the lightness, the brush of movement against my skin. Dancing, having something dancing around you to unite you in movement… Fabulous, fabulous indeed.' His face fell. 'Then I guess it all got packed away.'

'All packed away'. That was familiar and I was now beginning to realise just how much I too had packed away.

Fran was particularly fond of stroking my arms when I had my shirt sleeves rolled up and she would kiss me all the way up and make tunes between her lips with the hairs. She also loved to lie alongside me with her head on my chest when we were both naked and stroke it before playing with my chest hair, somewhat diminished now and grey. She never for a moment made me feel self-conscious or embarrassed about my age, our age difference, and by my, to me, often impossible adolescent inexperience of intimacy and sex. She could tease happily, and invite, with such subtlety and then all my old shyness, any awkwardness or fear left, just like that! Fran could invite me into her, and I could get lost. Lost in the smell, taste, scent, feel and sensation of her. Her touch always caused a shiver inside which was exquisite. I was experiencing freedoms I had started to experience with Frances but then completely banished. And now a new vista, a wide canvas of freedoms I had never known before. And at times feelings arose which I realised I had banned – jealousy. What would happen if Fran met someone else, someone her own age, or if she suddenly decided to return to Barcelona? I knew that she would have to return to Spain one day after she had completed her commission. What would I do? Would I get angry, frustrated, run after her, make a scene? Like an adolescent again? These thoughts were startling. Of course, we would one day have a conversation, as two adults about the future, and at times I dreaded it. The old voices arose: 'Don't be demanding, don't be naughty,' I heard myself say to myself. Naughtiness? What was it really? Against the tide, swim against the tide ...

'Just enjoy the moment.' Wisdom from my Buddhist understanding. I could interweave all those ancient understandings into the dynamics of these new experiences. And I laughed at myself, at my seriousness. It was never too late ... to have a happy adolescence or sex life!

Thinking about Agnes and reflecting on our work, I did, every now and then, allow myself to realise that I had at times become slightly irritated by Agnes' constant denial of her pregnancy, finding myself sceptical. How can it be that a child can gestate inside a body and the owner not know? I knew that it did happen, and research confirms this. But what had led Agnes to this level of unconsciousness. I pondered again on her account of the night in Cracow, a night of Eternity fragrance, a night which sounded as if it could have touched her in a significantly sensual as well as sexual way. Should I have asked more? More detail? I had not wanted to push it but after our recent and first spontaneous embrace initiated by her, I wondered there was something I had missed, some psychological technique. Why had she banned herself from allowing sexual pleasure, why was it so bad to enjoy herself in this way? But immediately I knew. This is exactly what I had done. I had banned all thoughts of my own sexuality after Frances. Sex, losing oneself in pleasure, orgasm, was dangerous. It led to awful things happening which had to be paid for. The price of guilt indeed. Is this the powerful drive that had rendered Agnes unable to listen to her body enough to acknowledge that she was pregnant. Complete and utter denial for that night in Cracow. Unless this was my projection of an old fear of real sexual and sensual experience.

It was smell, that fragrance of Eternity, that had awakened the memory of the one night Agnes had sex. Smell, of all the five senses was most closely connected to the brain. It was the power of that particular smell that ignited memory of the night of conception. We had shared the power of some of the other senses together: sound – music, birdsong, and voice – to touch feeling states, but we had yet to discuss taste or physical touch. I wondered whether she had any sense memory of touch, receiving it from another. Or whether this was something we could explore. And we had just shared a first natural and happy embrace. At the same time, I was aware of the paradox in psychotherapy: psychotherapists did not touch their patients unless there was an important reason to do so. This was startlingly telling I realised then, for to speak of touch is quite different from receiving it and noticing the many aspects of our body's reaction to touch.

After speaking about the dream, Agnes and Carole came together the following week. Agnes had brought a small pink bear. 'Carole found it in a charity shop,' she said. 'I love it.' We did not return to the dream as she was particularly taken by the fact that she had held her mother's hands. 'I've never done that before, and she has never held mine as far as I can remember. It was strange, really strange. But as I held them, I wanted more, curiously. You'd think, wouldn't you, that I would steer clear of her since she's always steered clear of me.'

Carole looked at her fondly and took her hands in hers.

'One thing though she did reveal when I asked her about her own birth, she went very quiet. I was about to say, 'Sorry,' but she shook her head and said very sadly, 'My mother died giving birth to me.' Agnes took a deep breath. 'I felt shocked and something in me shuddered at the parallel, but in the birth I missed consciously, it was my own child who died not me. If I have carried so much guilt since that, might it be the same if your own birth was the cause of your mother's death?'

I leaned forward. 'When your mother was born there was much less available for pregnant women and birth.'

She nodded. 'Yes, and they were refugees. I imagine that my mother was born in the Nissen hut. But it's made me think a lot more about guilt. How it impacts and is held. My mother is so held in, so withdrawn, so suspicious of ordinary life. What if she has spent her whole life feeling guilty? It's that magical guilt you speak of isn't it, a guilt for something we cannot possibly be guilty for, something so early and beyond our conscious awareness.'

Carole was looking at Agnes throughout, looking

impressed by her connections and understanding, as was I.

'Then, somehow, she gets pregnant herself, probably mistakenly, and when she was in her mid 40s, and she just blanks the whole thing out in case it all goes wrong. I've never felt closely connected to her, not like I've been able to do with Anna … but she did give me life, and a life, fed and watered, allowed to go to school and then, leave freely, sort of …'

Tears were not far away.

'And now we are beginning to talk …'

There was a long pause. Carole stepped in and said, 'At the weekend Agnes and I went back to Essex to see if the Nissen huts were still there from the post war years. And they were! They were in a bit of a sad state but we've since looked up on the internet lots of detail about the post-war conversion of MoD premises for Polish refugees. They were all over the UK. But of course, we would never be able to trace anyone from these times and Agnes' mother has no contacts from then. But Agnes and I could imagine her mother growing up there as a little girl, perhaps playing with other Polish children, going to school and church …'

Agnes looked at Carole fondly.

'It was a great idea to go. We took photos. When I see my mother next, I'll take some to show her. And, she added. 'I will go slowly, as you have with me, Doctor.' She looked at the clock. 'Would you play Chopin again? Perhaps the Nocturne in C- sharp minor?'

I smiled and stood up, I was now used to sharing music with Agnes and also at times with Carole. Despite concerns I might have had about my playing the piano as part of a therapy session I sat down, and my fingers moved easily over the keys. This was one of my favourite pieces, it reached right into the cells of my whole body, especially my heart with its wistful, gracious melody; its questioning trills. The three of us sat together receiving this gift from Poland's most famous composer.

Chapter 14

Dreams. The communication and language of the unconscious. I felt really pleased that Agnes had started dreaming again and that she had the resources now to record and share them. It felt brave.

I had asked her several times about the comments she made when we first met: 'She comes to me in my dreams.' And, 'How could you not know I was there. I wanted to land with you.' But she had shuddered and shaken her head, diving into the scarf. In all our work together, she was consciously trying to meet and reconcile herself with the reality of those hidden months of pregnancy and birth. I realised that the reality of there being a child inside her, let alone a being having a voice, and an intention, was overwhelming. It was huge to me. And mysterious. And yet this dream had got through.

The dream being who wanted to be with her had used the word 'land', which had so many associations. For Agnes expressed great aliveness when she was outside, near the lake, walking through the woods, watching the birds on the land and the water. The dream connected her to the land, a place where she felt she most belonged. The child she had carried was a presence in her unconscious world, with a voice. It made me curious to know more about what kind of voice she had, and if she had a name. I wondered also about all the lost children in Agnes' ancestral family, and whether some of their voices could live on through ancestral trauma.

In my reading about the horrific events at Birkenau I learned that the Nazi soldiers had tortured women who had become pregnant by them in the camp so that they miscarried. I had also read that more than 150 children were born in the camp, only a few of whom survived. There were what were called Children's Marches, where children were rounded up and had to walk naked to the gas chambers. One woman had given birth on the floor of the hut she shared with many others, and they all had cared for the carefully hidden new-born child until she was discovered by a Nazi soldier foraging in the dirty blankets. The child's presence had offered a beacon of light and the possibility of new life in this desperate community who faced starvation, torture and death every day. The scenes that followed her discovery were horrific. The shared shocked silence that follows such brutality is described with great compassion by Bernie Glassman. It is hard to find words that can honour such events. But honouring the experiences of those who had suffered by bearing witness to them, and to those who still suffer from persecution and segregation was an important offering.

It seemed that the wordless threads of these scenes are carried inside each person who has been witness to them, and continue inside each of whoever comes after them. The shared silence of most of the survivors of the camps also maintained these threads. And so a great silence was maintained. I hypothesised they could only be carried within, inside the fabric of the body, as a silenced body memory; and then continued inside each of the next generations and whoever came after them. The silences endured are repeated by the relatives who visit the site of their ancestors' suffering even many years later, their ancestors' experiences having never been able to be discussed or shared. They remained as deep ancestral trauma with no voice, hidden inside each one, and the studies of epigenetics were now beginning to offer clear understandings for this physicality. Agnes' mother had clearly suffered in this way, born to refugees who had been persecuted before managing to escape from Poland and kept to their learned safety of a lifelong silence, unable to find a voice to enquire.

I read again the inspiring work of Victor Frankl, Professor of Neurology and Psychiatry in Vienna who spent three years in Auschwitz and learned deeply about how, when faced with suffering, whatever system of acceptance, hope and meaning each individual is able to find within them, makes a huge difference to their attitude. This echoed my own studies of Buddhism, where all forms of life had to include suffering, and that true compassion arose from the acceptance of suffering.

Agnes' mother was born just after the war and possibly carried the great silence of these ancestral memories. This was communicated via her harshness, impatience and occasional cruelty, especially to fragile others over whom she had power, like Agnes. These behaviours could be seen as a way of fending off vulnerability, certainly of availability and openness so essential for life, and for love. Those never shown love find it hard to recognise it or offer it. I knew many people of my generation, post-war babies who had family members who had returned from either of the World Wars who could never speak of their experiences. They sat in silence, found any form of relaxation or receiving kindness impossible. In recent times the soldiers who had fought in Vietnam faced such hostility on their return that many of them limped off to live in the forests, unable to cope with a return to everyday life. They were silenced by the attitude of their countrymen and women who had not seen or endured what they had. There was no shared language for them to find any form of healing or peace however small. My work with soldiers returning from Afghanistan with PTSD had taught me so much about these great silences, the silence of unrecognised emotional pain; and how eventually it was possible to be present with such suffering and the way it lived on and to find new ways of being that were helpful.

Agnes was of another generation, one where perhaps an enquiring and creative voice and the capacity to find spaciousness and support could help in making the familial past visible, even in all its horror. I knew of groups who had formed themselves to share experiences where their impossible feelings could be recognised and held, made bearable if possible, and, when appropriate, to make offerings of peace and healing for all, for those no longer present or still hidden within their memories. I wondered also if Agnes' newfound way of communicating with her mother might unlock something vital, for I imagined that she must also be carrying so many unspoken feelings and memories, especially the attitude toward her and her displaced family in her desolate early years.

In the summer of our fourth year together, when Agnes was beginning to become more in touch with the different expressions of her body, I discussed with her the revelation she had about the child coming to her in her dreams. At first, she didn't respond, but then looked up and said, 'I need to be brave again, don't I?' We smiled together. 'Perhaps … If there was a child with a voice who wanted to visit perhaps, I could find a way to invite her to return.' She gasped. 'Not in the literal way you understand.'

I nodded and said, 'indeed … let's look at how you might seek this.'

She had folded her arms over her knees, looking at me coyly.

'Well, I didn't bring it up before because you might think we were being silly, but,' she looked definitely coy then and excited, 'Carole suggested that, as it was the summer months when I was pregnant' – I noticed how she now spoke the word easily – 'which is the time we're in now, I could pad myself out. She invented some padding for me to wear in my clothes and we've added to it as the months go on. She's studied these things you see.'

I was pleased for her and intrigued. I also wondered why I had not thought of this, and immediately scolded myself for my egotism. It was clearly important for Carole to find out as much as possible about a woman's body; she was deeply interested and involved, and I had admiration for this exploration. I smiled back. 'Good idea.'

Agnes looked relieved. 'I hoped you wouldn't think it frivolous.'

I shook my head. 'Tell me, Agnes, how is it going?'

'Well, we've just started. If the, my… gosh… baby…' she said these words slowly, bravely, 'was conceived in March, by September I could be six months pregnant. The baby, my baby, would have been due in December, a Christmas or pre-Christmas baby. But she was born in late October … at least two months premature.'

She suddenly slumped forward, sobbing in a way I had not experienced before. 'And –', in between sobs I heard, 'not living – not living, oh God, not living.' She was sobbing, wailing. It was eerie and heart breaking. I leant forward and offered to take her hands.

The following week she stood with her profile toward me. 'Can you see?' She patted her belly. I could see that she had indeed created a noticeable swelling of her girth with the padding provided by Carole.

'So how many months are you?' I asked lightly.

'Still a bit early, four maybe five I think.'

'Say how it feels'.

She shrugged. 'Not sure. It's certainly different, I am aware of it… I have to stand in different ways and when I sit down it's… something's definitely there … and I do find myself stroking my belly.' She looked suddenly really, really sad. 'But, but these are, were, just early days weren't they and no one else noticed. When would anyone notice? Some people hardly show… Anyway… what I've just described is only on the outside isn't it? I don't feel any different inside … and she, she, hasn't come to me again.'

Before the August break Agnes, Carole and I discussed the possibility of a return to Salisbury Plain on the same October day when six years ago Agnes' daughter was born there. It would be close to the anniversary of the beginning of our work together and as we started into our fifth and final year of therapy. I was uncertain at first but the two of them seemed keen and wanted to prepare, so I went along with what felt like an important journey. They wanted me to accompany them.

Throughout that summer they bought baby clothes and a Moses basket from charity shops and prepared for this incoming child with conscious determination. Agnes brought some of the clothes to the session just before we completed for the August break, and we held them between us; she raised some to her cheeks and at times wept into them. She intended to add more layers of padding as the weeks passed. At times she would look at me with her blue eyes so full of sadness. 'But I'm doing all this, I'm doing everything I can, aren't I, and it's all doing, not experiencing … nothing from my body. It's so weird, after all this time … but no memory. Nothing.' She would feel around her now large belly in despair.

Despite continuing with these explorations Agnes clearly had mixed feelings about going back to Salisbury Plan for the anniversary. I so admired her courage, to continue with this therapeutic journey that was both strange and curiously inviting to her. She was a young woman who never gave up. She had had so much suffering and come through it, to begin again, with such determination. And this continued even when it felt as if we were all – Carole included - venturing into areas of which we had no experience or even comprehension. It was all new, to all of us. And, now that I reflect back years later, each step became part of a process that changed each of us and our lives, internally and externally.

In an opposite vein to Agnes' continuing suffering and fears, I enjoyed a wonderful August break in Suffolk, spending most of the time with Fran. And, despite my awareness of the contrast I did allow myself to let go, completely. Fran was often at my cottage, which felt as if its' very fabric was also being given a new lease of life after all the sadness its walls had witnessed. How we played and revelled, danced and sang. We walked far along that Suffolk beach, sometimes on sand, often on pebbles; we walked into the waves together with Millie, her dog. We swam and played. We cooked together, fish from the stalls by the river in Southwold, salad leaves from the garden. We made bread, singing Spanish nursery rhymes Fran taught me, waving her stirring spoon in time to the beat; We sang together into the evening as I played the piano, old tunes from Schumann, sometimes so seriously until she laughed and began jiggling around. ' C'mon Maxie...lets rock...' then she would imitate 'Great Balls of Fire' from Jerry lee Lewis. One day she stepped into .... 'Fields of Gold', which made my heart leap. She had a good contralto voice. We danced; we drank good wine. She would read Lorca to me in both English and Spanish and invite me to speak in Spanish.

'You have good pronunciation' she said.' Muy Bueno.'

I did have moments when I wondered at the justice, fairness, I'm not sure, of my enjoying myself so much when Agnes was suffering. I would shake my head when I had these thoughts and scold myself for getting overinvolved. But it did also highlight how difficult it was for me to accept fully the treasures my life had brought to me in the face of the kind of loss one of my patients was enduring. So, having realised properly where these thoughts originated, I sent some good mindful energy in Agnes' direction, and I just got on with it all, this gift of new life, revelling in every moment. Loving it all.

Sometimes at dusk we would cycle up to Minsmere and enter the bird hides to watch the avocets as they flew in to settle for the night. We'd hear the owls call as we bicycled home at dusk. I had never known four whole weeks of such joy on so many levels. No responsibility, nothing of great weight, no 'must do's'. I wondered often whether I was intoxicated, and that what was happening, how I felt, was not real and one day I would wake up and find it all a dream. Or, worse, that Fran was all in my imagination, a starving elderly man led by the lifetime hunger.

I returned to London full of joy, a little sad, but knowing I would return to those Suffolk sands and that what I now carried was a real fund of energy and hope.

When Agnes and I resumed our sessions that September she was subdued. She came on her own at first, saying that she just wanted time to sit with me and reflect on what had already passed. She had had three reasonable visits to her mother. At one of them she asked her mother if anything remained from her early years as she had remembered that her mother kept some boxes on the top of her wardrobe. Her mother had just shrugged and looked away. But Agnes had once again reached out to hold her mother's hand and said, 'Have a look, on your own if you prefer. Or when I come next week, we could look together.'

And on that second visit her mother had indeed reached for the box, which she opened once Agnes arrived. There was a small rag doll, which her mother held against her chest and wept. There were three photographs. One was of her mother as a small child with someone she did not recognise, holding her hand. There was a picture of a Nissen hut. Her mother continued weeping. Agnes told her simply about what she was learning about her visit to Poland and how she was wanting to explore something of her ancestry. She told her mother that she knew it was deeply painful for both of them, but she wanted to be brave enough to know more, and to try to understand something of what her grandparents and she, her mother, had gone through. She had hesitated before including, 'I'd also like to find out about the child I conceived who I never knew … and I am doing my best …' Her mother had looked away muttering about shame.

Agnes had then taken a deep breath and a huge leap, which amazed me after how her mother behaved when she first found out about the child. She had said to her mother:

'I have a feeling that it is all related. And if I can release something of my own suffering perhaps I can also for you, Mother.' Her mother had evidently looked startled and pursed her lips in a familiar fashion before looking at her with eyes full of amazement. It was the closest communication she and Agnes had ever had.

On the most recent visit Carole had come with her and she introduced her to her mother. She said that Carole was 'amazing' and offered to help her mother with all kinds of chores, especially around the bird feeder on the balcony where weeds were growing around the dropped seeds. 'At least she's feeding them,' said Agnes, with some humour.

Chapter 15

I wanted to know and understand more about the call of Salisbury Plain for Agnes. I had been there twice with Emily on one of our rare excursions many years ago. On the last occasion she had noticed a couple of uniformed soldiers walking in the distance and stopped immediately, stamping her feet: 'There you go again, you bring me here for a nice day out and here are your bloody soldiers again.' My heart had sunk. She had already gone on about the work I was doing with soldiers, accusing me of bringing that energy into the house. Since then, I have realised that unconsciously I was indeed sabotaging that outing. It was one of the parts I played in the end of our marriage. This visit was shortly before she left, and we had the long break before our final parting and divorce. It all felt a long time ago. I did not miss her, just at times felt angry, with her and with myself. I wanted to clear myself of those unhappy associations, particularly now that I was discovering a new energy of life and a very different experience of being with a woman wholeheartedly, in real emotional, physical and sexual intimacy.

I knew well from my work with soldiers suffering PTSD, that many of them had trained on Salisbury Plain and then returned there after combat to be in one of the debriefing programmes conducted there. It was a place of great history on many levels, a place of extremes. I had decided, before leaving for my holiday weeks in Suffolk, that I would drive out from London and explore the Plain for myself and let any of my own painful memories dissolve into the dust of this ancient place. I also wanted to see if being there could uncover more questions for me to ask Agnes before we went there together. Agnes had also mentioned being there when she was very young with someone who was kind. It was certainly a place where there were reminders of past inspiration and greatness with its monuments to history and hidden artefacts in the dust.

Agnes was found near to the great stones of Stonehenge by a small slope. She was covered in wet sandy dust as she had been tossing and turning in it, and she was wet through from the rain. This much I learned from the notes taken after she was collected by ambulance. The description reminded me vividly of my friend Philip, who had a fatal heart attack whilst out walking and was also found by early morning walkers and their dogs. He also was found lying near a hedge on the slope of a ditch.

In exploring more about the history of Stonehenge, I discovered that it was originally thought to be an ancient burial site and I felt a slight shiver and some kind of recognition. Burial site. Was Agnes unconsciously trying to journey somewhere meaningful to give birth; were there moments when she suspected she might be carrying a child who was dead? Was it all the work of her unconscious, or the collective unconscious from her ancestors? It sounded far-fetched, as if I was grappling with bits of straw in the hope of making sense of this mysterious event. I also knew that throughout our years of working together I had not once had a glimpse that Agnes had any awareness at all of being pregnant, nor of giving birth. It was a truly momentous event to have blocked out so successfully.

Late in July I drove west towards this famous ancient site that I'd visited once as a part of a school trip and twice with Emily. It was a misty afternoon, I chose to pull off to the left and park where I could, on the edge of a footpath opposite the great stone pillars of history. I looked across at the ancient site, where I could see the small figures of the many walkers doing the circuit and wondered whether there had also been visitors there when Agnes arrived, but we had no idea of the time she might have got here or how long she might have lingered before she moved into full labour. All these words – pregnancy, labour, contractions, bleeding – which we had shared were still difficult for her. She spoke of them, but her body clenched, and her tone sounded formal and detached, not as feelingful as if the words came from within an embodied experience.

I stood for some time taking in all the sounds and smells of this mysterious place. I recognised the call of the corn buntings as I had heard them over the heath in Suffolk. There was little movement other than the walkers in the distance and the flight of rooks. A common blue butterfly hovered around me as I stood gazing. A gentle soul, fragile, reminding me of Agnes. The whole place had a mystery and eeriness and I wondered again about what it was that had called Agnes to it. She had spoken of it being the place where she had received kindness, a kindness that was new and had touched her deeply probably on many levels, with real feeling in body and mind. Was it this, kindness, that she was seeking for her child? And also, probably for herself. I also wondered about the music of the place, the calls, the echoes, the places of pilgrimage. I did not know if she knew about the army manoeuvres, or maybe Carole had mentioned something... we had not discussed it. I stood for some time taking in the sounds and wondered if she had heard the music and call of the place, perhaps in her dreams ... I could not place it, but perhaps over time and listening it would arise.

I crossed the busy main road and into the area near to Stonehenge and looked across at the vast stretch of the grasslands, still green, lying on their ancient chalk foundation. On the Plain, but away from here, I knew there were still many army manoeuvres carried out and occasional firing and many areas were forbidden to the public. I had discovered through my work with soldiers and PTSD that many of them were helped to release some of their body's trauma after returning from Afghanistan through coming to this very place where they had taken part in military exercises in preparation for combat, so the place had many associations and prior memories.

I also had a colleague who used to help to establish army rehabilitation exercises on Salisbury Plain. He spoke warmly of the meetings he helped to set up with exhausted soldiers wounded and traumatised, still suffering flashbacks, many of them reduced to silence and isolation. Some were living in tents on the Plain and elsewhere. The programme he worked on gathered these groups of soldiers together with experienced archaeologists. Each day they dug into the earth with their special tools as well as their hands and found treasures which they brought back to the camp for cleaning and examination. The archaeologists helped them to explore the origin and age of their finds and share ideas about earlier life here. The sharing of experience and speaking together, the enjoyment of shared meals as they became a team exploring hidden treasures helped to begin the process of healing. On some of the pottery pieces there were fingerprints from long ago. There were skeletons of animals. By returning them to the place where they had trained for battle to be differently reconciled with the earth and its capacity for regeneration, this process allowed them all to begin to experience release from their trauma, and a very different relationship with Salisbury Plain. He and I had spoken often whilst I was setting up the clinic for soldiers still suffering PTSD and I was researching different ways of working therapeutically. Frank Bright, who I remembered fondly and who was still in touch, was one of the soldiers referred by my army doctor colleague.

It was of course Agnes and Carole who had brought up the subject of going to Salisbury Plain on the anniversary of the birth and invited me to join them. I pondered on this for a while and discussed it with a trusted colleague who wondered whether this was wise. He suggested that either I encouraged them to go, or, just Agnes and I went to lend it some more therapeutic authority. I would be the only container of whatever transpired; it would be more like a therapy session outside of the consulting room. I thought about it for quite a while before speaking to them both about how it might be to do this unusual activity. I told them about the traumatised soldiers and the excavation work they had done on the Plain together with professional archaeologists. How they all discovered long buried fragments. I explained how taking up a voyage together, hands in the earth, finding buried treasure, discussing it as a group and then sharing food and conversation together had brought much healing to this group. Agnes was fascinated. I emphasised the therapeutic part of this journey, one that needed firm boundaries and containment, which meant that it was important for just Agnes and I to go together. I could tell that Carole was really dejected as she had so wanted to be part of it. But she had had therapy and knew the process well and was respectful. She would be waiting for us at her flat on our return.

Agnes and I left London in my car soon after 6 a.m. one Saturday in early October. We travelled slowly and in silence. It felt a huge and momentous event, for both of us. We were venturing into the unknown. We left London in darkness, the houses lining the M4 dimly lit, the M25 strangely empty of traffic. As the dawn began to rise and we left houses and buildings behind us I wondered if we might experience another dawn, that fresh light might arise for Agnes on the birth of her child. It was a simple journey on one level but carried with it heaviness and uncertainty and a fear of too much expectation. I had said, many times, 'This will be an experiment together, please don't expect much. We will share whatever arises. We are offering the possibility of new light on your pregnancy and your child's birth.'

Carole had already helped her to visit the hospital where she was taken all those years ago, and they had both read the admission notes, so they knew the exact date and location where the ambulance was sent. Agnes thought that she had probably hitched lifts all the way from her mother's flat in Brixton and walked towards Stonehenge after being dropped off in the nearby village. We imagined together that her contractions must have been getting more regular and painful. She clutched at her stomach area when I named this. She must have crossed the main road and walked into the Stonehenge area and lain down.

On this October morning, six years after the birth, Salisbury Plain was shrouded in mist when we arrived. We initially stopped on the side of the road and looked across at the view through the mighty pillars of Stonehenge. It was simply beautiful, as mysterious as the stones, and empty, without visitors walking through. The stone curlew and other rare small birds had been seen here alongside the gentle butterflies. The great bustard was also often seen here, a huge figure in the landscape and a great survivor. This was a place of vast contrasts. Prehistoric finds in the earth still preserved in the chalk, ancient monument to human ancestors, walkers looking for country release and the regular army, who still had most of the walking rights on large areas of the Plain and exercised here in full military kit.

I couldn't see Agnes' face as she sat beside me, but I could sense her tension and fear. I felt for her deeply and I wondered, many times that morning, whether it was wise to attempt such a journey, and what might emerge from it. I could see that she was trying to keep her eyes open but some of the time shielded any view with her Cracow scarf. I knew that this helped her to feel protected. Through the open weave of the knitting, she could see just enough to tolerate.

We had to turn off the main road further away from

the Stones and park in the visitor area. Agnes had become frozen and mute, so we sat for a while, taking in the sight and sounds around us and practised some slow mindful breathing. Eventually we ventured out, standing still at first and taking in the smells and feel of the place. She needed my help to walk over the heath so that we could enter the area near Stonehenge itself. It was Agnes' suggestion that initially we walk around this great ancient monument which could help us to be truly present in the place. It might also help there to be more conscious memories of seven years ago at this time, in this place. For Agnes was now much more aware of her different senses. I hoped that the sounds, feel and smells of the place would be helpful for memory. She was pale and silent, hands over her stomach. Carole had encouraged her to strap the padding onto her abdomen at about the level of a seven-month pregnancy.

We walked for about 45 minutes, away from the stones at first and then returning to them, Agnes leading the way. From time to time, I would look toward her and saw that often she had her eyes closed. I noticed that she kept her hand on her belly as I had suggested, to help keep her in contact with the intention of this visit but also to help her regulate her breathing as she was walking. She had found this practice very useful in her everyday life and had even written a chant to go with it, which she used silently several times a day. She had also sung the chant to me beautifully and we had practised it together. I was so moved to see her there, marvelling at her level of attention and acutely aware of her suffering.

Just before 10 o'clock the sky seemed to darken, and I wondered if it might rain. I was amazed and relieved that no visitors had yet come to the Plain. I looked up. A storm, thunder and lightning would indeed be dramatic on this anniversary day. Suddenly a group of black rooks appeared out of the darkening sky, as silent as the dawn had been. They began to settle on some of the stones not far from us, nodding their heads and preening their feathers between their loud squawks.

I turned to look at Agnes, who was standing very still with her hands over her ears and her eyes opened wide. She began turning round and round in circles making a strange buzzing sound … bzzz … bzzz … as if she were a wasp. I went toward her wanting to help her, to offer protection, but she pushed me away. 'No, no!' she screamed at the top of her voice, her eyes closed … and again covered her ears with her hands and continued running round and round in circles, away from the stones. I tried again to reach her and comfort her but was brushed off. 'No, no,' she screamed, 'no, no … get off me, get off me …' She ran forward, her hands remaining over her ears, and as I stood still she screamed at me in a tone I had never heard before, harsh, alien, 'get away, get away! You find out all about me, get me to trust you, and then … you're here to torture me. I know … I know… ! You get me all vulnerable, find out things and then you bring me here to finish me off.' Her face was contorted into something like a snarl, her breathing rapid and shallow, she spat on the ground. 'Torturers, torturers the lot of you and you're not going to get me. Get away, get away!' And she ran, as fast as she could, away from me onto the Plain.

I felt deeply shocked. Deeply sad. What was it I was seeing, witnessing? I had not foreseen this and was immediately angry with myself for not realising that she might have some incredibly difficult experiences here on the Plain, and so might I. But what was it she was seeing or uncovering? I ran after her, carefully keeping a reasonable distance as she kept looking back at me, sticking her tongue out and shouting. Then, as the rain pelted down she seemed to disappear. It was hard to see and for me the moment was terrifying. Where had she gone? I wondered whether she was behind one of the stones.

I tried to breathe deeply and slowly. I had to find her. I knew enough from my work with many people, soldiers especially, that she would be suffering from shock, and that being here would have brought back memories from many avenues in her life including her recall of Cracow and the camps. I just had not anticipated what form her shock might take. There was also of course the delayed shock at the whole experience of finding out she had been pregnant of which she had been completely unaware and that she had, here, in this very place, given birth to a daughter. I feared for what she might do to herself in the heat of such deep shock.

I had brought some piano music on my phone with me, one of her Chopin favourites, which she and I both thought of as possibly being healing and we had listened to it together many times. I remained near the stone where I had last seen her and turned up the volume. I thought about what she had told me so far about her recent discoveries of her family history, particularly her mother's family and their experiences in Poland during the war. I thought about the way that this history had been silenced during her mother's life but now, through Agnes' courage, some of it was being uncovered. And there was the experience in Cracow after visiting Birkenau, of Agnes letting go sexually, sensually, losing herself in the joy of intimacy and embrace as I was now doing with Fran. For her, it was an intimacy which resulted in the conception of her child and for which there was, possibly, deep hidden shame. Perhaps shame at having pleasure after witnessing such horror and death.

And I thought about the dream she had had, of being a child imprisoned and looking through the cracks in the wooden enclosure. Looking at torturers, at torture. She was indeed a silently tortured young woman, constantly fighting internal demons but at the same time bravely taking on much in the outside world. But these internal voices had never been voiced and heard. I had sensed them but not heard them in the safety of my consulting room. But here they were now.

The rooks were still circling, like the voices inside Agnes. I lifted my head toward the sky and let the rain fall onto my face. I kept my thoughts onto Agnes, of her suffering and all the suffering of her family. I thought of her child, and the child who visited her in her dreams, wanting to land, 'to land with you'. If I was praying, I prayed for this journey we were on to help her find the safest conscious awareness and also healing.

It continued to rain. I walked in the direction I had last seen her, the music still playing. Then I heard gentle singing coming from a low bushy area and found Agnes lying still, singing to herself quietly, and weeping, holding something in her arms. She was wet through, her face and arms shiny with rainwater. She had pulled out the padding she had strapped around her waist which held the tiny pink bear and she was stroking it in between stroking her abdomen. She was holding a small vial of water.

She looked up. 'Ah there you are … at last … I've been

waiting for you. I've seen them off, they've gone, Doctor. Those horrors, those awful voices that would destroy life, any hope of proper life ... life you and I have spoken of ... And look! I've found her, found her at last ... here she is. Can you see her, how beautiful she is? And there's the special water I brought... I'm christening my daughter with this special water ... her name is Hope.'

Chapter 16

Hope. This simple word, its one-syllable sound, its many associations, filled the atmosphere in the car as we drove back to London. No need for other words. Hope. No need to interpret or analyse, no need to discuss. The word itself came at the culmination of an extraordinary morning and had awakened both of us to some new awareness we needed to be with silently. The word created a shivering I sensed in both of us. Shivering within the wordless threads we were weaving together. A present moment felt sense of knowing, rather than a memory. This was accompanied by the sharing of a profound experience. I drove slowly, aware of all of this and the sense of both of us savouring the whole experience which culminated in that word. Hope. I held the word inside my heart, sounded it silently, felt it in my solar plexus and in my hands as I softened them against the steering wheel.

Hope. Agnes nursed the bundle that had been wrapped over her abdomen on our outward journey. It felt as if she was at last bringing the reality of her child into her life. The child born six years ago who had called to her in her dreams she had today christened Hope and was bringing her home. Every now and then she would say in a very low voice, 'I've found her, I've found her,' and she would sing what sounded like a lullaby, possibly in Polish. She would also say directly to the small bundle, 'I've found you, found you … I've been looking for you … trying to …' Every now and then she would reach over to touch my hand. 'Thank you, thank you'.

I was moved by this latter experience and at the same time still unnerved by the squawking monster that I had represented to her earlier. And of course, curious psychologically for although it was a form of transference, it was also much more than that. I liked to think that our work together had prepared her to face her monsters and she had done so. It was in these moments of recollection that I allowed thinking to take over to ponder on the two opposites. Relational gratitude, and intense fear creating hate. I could also think about how we both shared these two opposites, love and hate. We could love another from a distance and give out to others, but that which we feared and had to placate was silenced and left unexplored. Perhaps we were both in flight from the oppressors in our own psyches, running from feeling bad, filling every moment. Helping others rather than ourselves.

But I knew that it was too soon to let thinking and analysis take over, however much I was tempted to be analytic and disappear down this route thinking that there are opposites in all of us! But with awareness we can recognise and reconcile them, so they are not split off and become demonic figures possessing us and taunting. I was having very new relational experiences in my own life, and I wanted this new opening to help me to stay with the feeling and the felt sense of that day. It was clear that something extraordinary had happened and was still happening.

I also knew this was not the only avenue needed. That this was a pivotal moment in the therapy was clear. So many threads were coming together.

Carole was waiting for us at the flat. It seemed an age since she had waved us off that morning. 'Look, look,' called Agnes, 'I've found her, here she is. Her name is Hope.'

I watched them stand together admiring the bundle. Agnes was reluctant to put Hope down but eventually, after Carole had made tea for us all, she placed her on the sofa between herself and Carole. She took a deep breath whilst stroking her now flat abdomen.

'What was it like?' asked Carole.

Agnes took a while to respond, sipping her tea and not making eye contact.

'All that time ago she came to me in my dreams. She said to me, 'I wanted to land, to land with you.' She looked up at me. 'When I came to see you, I said, 'How could I not know she was living inside me?'

Those still haunting words. The silence in the room was profound, some great moving revelation was happening. 'Well, now she has landed. She is here, by my side.'

The silence continued, all of us enveloped within our own responses to this huge awakening and what was being revealed. And also, what might come next. I had to stop my professional mind continually analysing, thinking about practicalities like integration and meaning. Agnes was coming down to earth with the reality that her child was dead. No form of hope could change that. So what would hope be about ... I had to stop my mind racing, following Eliot in The Wasteland ... the faith the love and the hope are all in the waiting... It was too soon to begin thinking about how all this got integrated into everyday life. Possibly ten or fifteen minutes went by as we drank our tea and pondered on what was continuing to unfold. Then Agnes said, 'there were monsters out there all right ... black monsters circling and torturers ... but I got rid of them. I shouted at them, called them by their true names and then I fled. They didn't come after me.' She looked at me in wonder. 'Why was that Doctor? Why did they not follow me?'

I smiled, allowing myself to be baffled. This was Agnes' experience, I wanted to let it unravel in her own way.

'What monsters?' asked Carole, alarmed. 'God, Agnes, were you in danger?'

'There were sadists out there, persecutors and torturers. They were circling, making horrible noises.'

I was intrigued to hear that she had such a clear recollection of these moments. To me, and clearly, it had been her unconscious that was projecting cruel sadistic monster forms. Possibly forms she had envisaged during her visit to Cracow but also possibly inside her mother, silenced by the fears these past monsters could inflict.

'But I saw them off.' Agnes was clearly thrilled that it was she who had managed this feat.

Carole asked, looking at me puzzled, 'Where were you then, Max, did you see them also?'

I pondered on how best to reply and said, 'There was a lot of noise from the rooks circling and Agnes shouted at them to stop. She was extremely brave having found her voice and her inner protector. You were amazing, Agnes.'

Carole looked intrigued. 'Rooks ... hmmm. You know, Agnes, this all reminds me – at a really low point during my army service, I saw monsters one day too, in the scrub land in Helmand province, which had suddenly become a battlefield. We were all taken by surprise ... But no one else saw them ...

it was hell. I was alone with them.' There were tears in her eyes.

Then she said quietly, her eyes shining and looking at me, 'It's him, because he was there. His presence drove them away.'

I was shocked and alarmed by this and its projection.

'I'm so sorry, Carole. I do remember your telling me about this time when you saw monsters and were alone ... I'm so sorry ... and now', I looked at Agnes, 'now it's time to share this together. It was you, Carole, who had the courage to continue with those monsters being there ... you had to fight them off and you did, like Agnes has just done. You are both such brave warriors. But today, ... it was Agnes who had the courage to name the monsters, say no to them and drive them away. I was glad to be there as a witness, but this is her own journey.'
I looked at Agnes in a friendly way and tried to be light-hearted. 'Salisbury Plain and all its memories and ghosts for you, Agnes, was your own experience. Please own it. This is how far you've come on this long journey. This is just the beginning.'

She was quiet and thoughtful.

'Yes,' she agreed, 'I can see that.'

'Tell me how you are feeling?'

She was very quiet. 'Right now, I feel full up. There's a lot I need to think about and – to use your words – process.' We all smiled. 'All this, today, it's huge. A lot to digest and take in.'

'Yes, it is. You've had a huge experience, Agnes. One that will, as you say, need to be processed. And there is no hurry. Carole and I will be there by your side. And Anna also I am sure, when you are ready to speak with her and share.' I was struck by the radiance on Agnes' face and wondered about it. 'Perhaps you could write something about today whilst it is still fresh. We can look at it together when you come for your next session. But for now, what do you most need?'

She looked at Carole. 'If it's OK with you, Carole, I should like to stay here, with you. And,' she looked down, 'with Hope, with my new life. I need to go slowly, to rest.'

Carole looked very happy. 'I will make you a bed up in here on the sofa. We will sit with Hope and then we will cook food together. We can play together on the keyboard. And sing! Those lullabies, the Chopin. We will choose music to welcome

Hope and welcome you here my dear, dear friend. We might even dance together.'

All this sounded good, and I was relieved that she would have support and be with someone who had been through so much trauma herself. I left the flat with mixed feelings. I was pleased to have been part of this journey with Agnes and clearly something quite momentous had happened which I was witness to. But where would we go next? How might Agnes feel in the morning? Or when she returned to her own flat and her everyday life. Where would her attachment go next after the bundle she had held so close to her body. There were even moments when I wondered whether my going along with the planning of this trip and its potential re-enactment was wise. Was I too much on a high having discovered my own expansion of new experience, especially within my physical body. My exhilaration had at times filled my whole being. I was perhaps guilty of 'try anything, you can't lose' or 'we are on a roll, let's go with it. You never know what it can bring. Look on the bright side.' Overall, I did allow myself to feel grateful to have had such a moving day. Also, I had no idea of what was to come.

Before I saw Agnes again, I had a few days to digest what had happened, to ponder more on the events on Salisbury Plain and how they unfolded experientially. We had gone with the unknown, without expectation. As we walked around Stonehenge, standing still to gaze across at the mighty stones and the open Plain beyond, some wordless process had begun to unfold. It was as though something slipped into place, without word or instruction, like a camera lens coming into focus. The images were still forming themselves in Agnes' psyche and we could not know yet where they would take us.

I remembered vividly the sudden harsh call of the rooks, and how disturbing they were to both of us. On my return to my own home the sounds, feelings, images of the day returned to me personally. I recalled Messiaen's birdsong, the opening sequences of notes. It was chilling, and real. I wondered about the felt sense response to the rooks within Agnes' body and whether she might have a memory or be able to encounter it again. All her private demons in those screeching calls, the darkness of the shapes. What voices did she hear, what aspects of possible ancestral past revisited her?

My first night home I dreamed of birds circling, I was unsure whether they were all rooks, they looked as if there were several different kinds of large birds. And those words appeared in the circling, the words of Agnes' child in her dream: 'I wanted to land with you.' But this was my dream and so I pondered more on the child I did not know that Frances was carrying, the child she never allowed to land for either of us. And all the other aspects of new life - what had I allowed to land within me, and what had I not. What potential new life had I suffocated and why. Was it all developmental? Old patterns of survival? An overwhelming sense of duty? A fear of doing wrong and being punished? Was I the good placatory clever boy that Frances called me? Untutored, naïve and after the first bite of reality scarpering in terror. Had I spent all these years living through other people's experiences, other people's suffering and not taking on my own? I woke with a shudder.

I sat outside drinking tea and allowed the soft autumn oak leaves to fall gently around me. It was good to remember that so much of what was happening between me and Agnes was shared experience, often accompanied by a felt sense in the body that was neither entirely somatic nor emotional in character. There was a particular energy in those subtle inner shifts and shudderings. It was also all in the present moment rather than a memory. Again those haunting words, which I still hear now, 'How could you not know I was living inside you?'

I next saw Agnes a few days later. I had not heard from her since our visit to the Plain. She was carrying the bundle of 'Hope' still and settled her down carefully on her lap before looking up.

'Well, Doctor. Here I am and here is Hope.' She smiled, still the radiant smile.

'How have these last few days been?'

She laughed, 'Domestic, playful. Carole and I played tunes and made them up. We danced; we cooked lovely food. We held Hope together.' She looked suddenly sad. 'I do know, I do know it's not the whole picture. I do know I've been on some magical adventure in the last months and that I will come to ground before long. Have to face reality … I do know this.' Her voice had dropped into seriousness. As I saw it, I felt a sudden relief.

I spent the following weekend with Fran. We also played music, danced, cooked and made love, over and over. I felt the sensation of real joy coursing through my body, a shivering thrill of equal measure tingling in my head, chest, arms, belly, pelvis, making my legs shake. However many times we had already engaged like this it was always as if it was the first time, which continued to thrill and amaze me. We walked through the woods that shivered with leaves falling and along the beach, Millie diving into the waves and looking back to see if I might join her as I did on that wonderful day when we all met. I was tempted to dive in, but Fran was holding on to my arm firmly, nibbling my ear from time to time. 'Too cold.'

I laughed. 'But I know ways we can warm up.' And we laughed together running along the strip of sand.

She knew that I had been doing something important on Salisbury Plain, but I had not discussed it with her. It felt so important to keep our time together with all its playful joyousness quite separate from work.

Fran had always laughed at my seriousness, particularly at the way I took myself so seriously. She would say, 'lighten up, Dr Max. You've got to learn to have fun. Not everything needs such earnestness.' But that weekend I found myself telling her something about the journey Agnes and I were making. Although I knew she would guard what I told her carefully for she had great respect for therapy, I tried without too many disclosures to tell her something of what had happened on Salisbury Plain. She stopped on the sand and looked serious suddenly. 'What a strange phenomenon … not knowing you are pregnant. Weird.'

'Well,' I laughed playfully, 'you would always know. You know your body so well. You are one with it.'

She was quiet. 'Know?' She looked suddenly serious. 'Alas conocimiento…To not know, with what do we know these things? What is that knowing, Dottore, where does it come from indeed?' I could see that she was still being serious. I held her close.

When she finally spoke, it was in a serious voice, quiet. 'I was pregnant once. I knew it, every day I knew it, and every day I wondered what I should do … but I did nothing. She shrugged her shoulders. I guess I was denying it wasn't I, pretending if I took no notice it would go away … I don't know what I would have done if I'd gone full term. She took a deep breath. Five months and then I lost her. She was a girl also.'

'Ah, dear Fran. I'm so sorry.'

She shrugged. 'It was a long time ago. I could never have kept her could I? I was still at university, in my last year.' She took a deep breath. 'Perhaps I had a close encounter. I knew all right, I knew I was pregnant – I even took a test. But I was ambivalent about this new life inside. I made no relationship with her. I was probably trying, by avoiding, to pretend it wasn't there and hope the whole thing would go away.'

I held her close to me and, for the first time felt her sorrow. And I was shocked. What else did I not know about her?

'Did the father know,' I asked slowly.

She laughed, more harshly than she had before. 'God no, he was my tutor, married, all that.'

I reeled. The patterns we shared. I had never told her about Frances.

'Let's go home, light a fire and make some delicious pasta,' I said. She smiled. Thoughtful.

On our return to the cottage, I saw a bicycle propped up on the wall. A young woman was trying the door. She appeared to have a bunch of keys. I stopped shocked.

'You've got a visitor,' said Fran, curious.

The woman turned round. I would never forget that face, that look, the expression of quiet desperation. I stopped, horrified. But why, after all these years? And here?

'Hello, Max,' she said. I stood still and closed my eyes. Fran turned to me, questioning.

'It's Emily,' I said eventually.

Chapter 17

Emily. After all these years. What was she doing here? More scary was what did she want? I was surprised that I had this thought. I was plunged straight back into fear, into duty, responsibility, the old patterns Emily triggered in our early days.

Instead of greeting her I said, probably harshly, 'What are you doing here?'

She laughed unpleasantly, 'Huh, that's not much of a welcome. I was your wife,' looking at Fran all the time. 'Aren't you going to introduce me?' She put her hands on her hips.

I felt Fran stiffen. I had told her only a little about my years with Emily, but I had told her that we were divorced. I wanted to say, 'You are my ex-wife,' with the emphasis on the ex... But I allowed myself a good breath remembering that Emily, despite her bid for independence after our years of marriage, still needed handling gently or ... or what I asked myself ... and now, after all this time. I was frustrated with my old patterns around her and at the same time torn. I just said, 'I thought you were living in Devon.'

She shrugged, saying nothing, so I had no idea what might have happened. She had the same pout she had during our early days, the same glare. In that moment, standing close to the warmth of Fran, I allowed myself to loathe her, the Emily she had been for so many years; and loathe the self I inhabited then in that long, empty, lonely marriage. I was surprised by my strong feelings! She then looked toward the cottage. 'I see you've kept it then. I thought you probably would.'

I breathed in deeply. Fran was starting to pull away. I turned to her and said quietly, 'It's fine, please stay. It's fine.'

'I'm obviously very surprised to see you, Emily, after all this time – what must it be, at least three years or more since we've had any contact?' I spoke weakly but really wanted not to be trapped into guilt and shame. 'I wish you had let me know you were coming,' I said quietly, but firmly, startling myself somewhat.

Still, she did not speak but just stared, at me, and at Fran. Hostile. And, something else, something sad. I wondered if she had become depressed again. But I was determined to press on keeping good boundaries.

'Like you, I now have another life. If you wanted to see me, why didn't you write, telephone, let me know?'

Fran remained still, her arm around mine. She said quietly, 'Is this something you need time together to discuss?'

'No, absolutely not.' I gestured toward Emily saying, 'Emily, I have a feeling that you want to speak with me about something. And I am wondering. If you wanted to see me, why not come to London. Easier from Devon.' I looked at her steadily. 'Are you are still living in Devon?' I had a sudden dread that she was homeless and thought she could be looking to move back in with me.

She remained staring, first at me and then at Fran. It would certainly be a surprise for her to see me with another woman. Still, she was silent. I stumbled on, annoyed with myself for not being clearer, more forceful, not sending her packing... But that had never, ever, been my way. I was fumbling, struggling to find some point of contact. But I could see it was impossible.

"How is your Shirley, is she alright? I remember how happy you were moving in with her.'

I remained standing near to the entrance to the cottage, and close to Fran who had remained and was standing very still. It felt wonderful to have her by my side at a moment like this.

Emily remained silent, sullen and, it felt, hostile. She looked just the same. Her body slightly bowed; she could have been that same forlorn young maiden-like creature I had met all those years ago in the Swiss mountains. The maiden I had decided to rescue from an institution after all her years of torment, and as a way to control the impossible feelings I knew only later I was carrying from my own years of torment and failure. Rescue? Whatever was I thinking, doing …. what was it exactly driving me then? I knew of course, but somehow seeing her again having discovered Fran my choice of Emily seemed bizarre and the self I was then seemed a long way away.

I watched her with determination, feeling the energy inside wanting to stand up to her, to not be bullied by her mood. There was that familiar sly half look as she turned her head, plotting something maybe. Just looking at her, it seemed as if she had regressed from the more positive Emily who had left me and gone to live with another woman. She even initiated our divorce, which had surprised me but by then I was pleased she had been brave enough to do it, and I think her new partner was insisting on it. I never knew whether they had had a formal arrangement. But again, I thought, why had she come back here? What did she want? From me of all people. Did she think I was still such a pushover?

It seemed as if we had all been standing there for ages. And I began to wonder, with some horror, if she still had keys and if she had, whether she had even been inside the cottage, she knew it well enough. Maybe she had been keeping a lookout waiting for me to leave the place. Was I paranoid? I had thought that some books had been moved, and my desk drawer opened, but I didn't think much of it at the time, knowing my own untidiness. My mind began really racing then, racing – what might she have been looking for? And if she had been in, she must have keys still.

We had gone through everything together and divided our shared assets. The cottage was always mine and the things there were from my parents. Emily had, it seemed, always respected the place and what it meant to me. She didn't always accompany me on my weekends when I was likely to be walking or meditating, preferring to stay in London with her needlework.

My mind was going furiously on and on, had she been looking for my diaries, for I used to keep one in notebook form, detailing many thoughts and ideas as well as events.

I was shocked afresh, for I could imagine her secretly holding on to a spare key, as a sort of keepsake, a memory of a place she knew I loved. There were also footsteps in one of the flowerbeds, small ones which I had thought were children for there were children in the house nearby. My mind continued reeling.

'Emily, I'm wondering whether you've been here before, when I wasn't here. Have you?' Still she was silent and sullen. 'And, if you still have keys, Emily, please give them to me. Now.' I was really firm with her, trying to keep eye contact. 'The keys Emily. I am sure you can understand that both of us need to respect our privacy in our new separate lives.'

She pouted. I decided to get nearer to her, and she

flinched. A great deal had happened between us, but we had never come to blows. Whatever had happened between her and the other woman?

I had to be assertive. I would not be trapped into guilt and shame. And I needed to do it for myself, but also for Fran. And, a sudden thought, yes! I needed to be assertive and positive for whatever future Fran and I might have. I had not thought of this before, it sent a thrill through my whole body.

'If you would like us to have a conversation, please let's speak tomorrow, when I am ready.' I turned toward Fran. 'Eleven o'clock tomorrow OK for you?'

Fran smiled, a beautiful smile. 'Buenos dias. That's a good time, yes.'

I turned back to Emily saying firmly... 'Please Emily, give me the keys now... keys. You have no right to them.'

She began fumbling in her bag. Eventually she found the keys to both back and front doors. She pulled them out and held them close to her chest.

'You were supposed to look after me, always.'

My heart sank. What on earth had brought this on? And what should I do about it if anything? The old tug of guilt was there all right, despite my last surge of firmness. She was being completely irrational, and I felt shocked ... had I missed something important ... but I was also furious, furious in a physical way I had not been aware of ever. This was what I imagined real rage was like. Furnace-like heat in the chest, bile in the mouth making me want to spit, all my muscles were clenched. Is this what I had been suppressing? Oh God ... all this time.

She looked harshly at Fran. Then back at me before throwing the keys on the ground.

'It's alright for you.' She spat out. 'So, I have to make an appointment do I, doctor. Doctor Max.' She sniffed. 'It's alright for you. It's always been alright for you, precious bloody Dr Max Maxwell.' She was sneering. 'I can see you've looked after yourself then. Place in London still, cottage by the sea.' She sniffed. 'A girlfriend – or, or are you the wife ... watch out I tell you, watch out for him, Dr too-good-to-be-true Max.'

Fran spoke to her gently. 'We have actually only just

met.'

I decided to be firm.

'Emily, we surely sorted out everything each of us needed when we made our separate arrangements. At the time you said they suited you well in your new life. We agreed our finances...'

She cut me off. 'You. You don't understand, do you? You just don't understand. Well, aren't you the lucky one.' And she actually spat on the ground. Then she got on her bicycle and as she cycled off turned her head and said, 'See you tomorrow then ... if... if I'm still here.'

For a split second I considered running after her, but she pedalled away fast, leaving her lethal threat to hang in the air.

I watched her disappear down the hill into the village. I'd been holding my breath. Then I realised that Fran had both her arms around me, and I felt her intention and strength pouring into me. It was the first time I felt supported by another being in the midst of impossible demand and I felt overwhelmed. I began weeping as we went into the cottage.

'I'll pour you a stiff drink,' she said.

I felt stunned and needed to compose myself. Lighting the fire was a good practical next step. As I bent twigs and placed logs, I began to light the flames and considered the extremes of helplessness and fire blazing inside myself. Those taunting words, 'watch out for him, Dr too good to be true Maxwell.' Reminding me of Agnes shouting as the rooks were circling... 'get off me...'

The shadow appearing, many shadows.

I hadn't thought of Emily for years. I had blessed my luck, for if she hadn't left me, I would never have left her. Never dared to. She'd had such a hold over me – duty, honour, guilt, and what Philip would call my 'saviour complex'. Damn it, damn it.

I could not let her sudden presence draw me into all that old stuff. And I did not want to lose Fran, who I was aware was now looking at me thoughtfully and in a new way.

And that final threat, 'If I'm still here'. Should I have run after her? Was that what she wanted? For me to 'save' her after all these years, save her again? To help her pick up the pieces from whatever had happened in Devon. And for what? My life was now completely different. I inhabited it differently. There was no place for Emily anymore.

'Tell me about her,' said Fran quietly.

My heart sank. What to tell? Those years, those years of being dragged down, the suppressed fury on my part, the duplicity, Emily's open and sullen hostility once I began working with soldiers, her verbal attacks. But there were also the early years when I felt I had a precious jewel to look after, to love. How arrogant I was! But yes, her gratitude and grace in the early years were a gentle tonic. And I had a wife. And during the years she had in therapy she appeared to grow more thoughtful. I felt that our lack of physical closeness and intimacy was a small price to pay. Having not been able to save my sister I had at least contributed to Emily's life. How ignorant I was!! How shocking. I wondered what had happened to all the reflective work she had done with her difficult past. I really didn't want to be thinking about her. But thoughts kept coming. On and on, like tormentors, like those circling rooks.

Seeing her here again it felt as if she was no longer the more mature self-aware woman she had become at the end of our marriage. The independent woman who was ready to be free and make different relationships from the one person who had 'rescued her' from life in an institution. A complete mystery indeed. Those years of celibacy, heaviness, my occasional irrational fear of being attracted to someone else … a patient even … The separate rooms – Fran would hardly believe that … and yet …. perhaps she would.

Eventually I started talking; I sank back into the chair and enjoyed the warmth of the fire and the soothing of the brandy. Fran was a good listener. There she was, as well as my fantastic sexual and sensual liberator she was a humane, mature and thoughtful listener. She would help me to find a voice. She would help me to find a voice to name some of what was happening.

'You mean you were celibate all through this marriage?'

'Yes,' I said very quietly, embarrassed 'Yes I was.'

She laughed and patted my knee.

'Hard to believe that the way we've known each other. But all that pent up stuff inside you, all that on hold and all because of what … the death of your sister?'

I realised I had never told her about Frances. There were things both of us had not shared as we kept our moments full of light and laughter, play and dance. She had told me only today about her pregnancy. An affair with her tutor. I now wanted to know more, more detail of what Fran had been through emotionally. And I wanted to tell her my affair with Frances and the child, the lost child. We were entering some of the grittier aspects of our past, it needed a place within our continuing passion and enjoyment. There was space enough for grit to find a place within the joys we shared. I realised I'd not spoken at all about the complexities of my past, and now I really wanted to. I no longer wanted to hide the harsh realities, they had to find inclusion for both of us.

I smiled. 'Here is what we share, dearest, darling Fran. I also had an affair, in my last year at Oxford. My tutor's wife …'

She listened, allowed me full vent of my times with Frances at Oxford – she raised her eyebrows when I said the name 'Oh la' she said…' surprised you didn't run a mile when you met another Fran.'

I closed my eyes as I spoke of these times and since, allowing all my regrets, my joys. She gave me such freedom; she did not judge. I could speak freely in a way I never had before. I told her about the glorious nights and days that Frances and I stole together. She enjoyed hearing this and squeezed my leg and kissed my mouth.

'Yes, express and enjoy. You've not forgotten it have you, even after all the years of hiding in terror…' And she hugged me and kissed me again. 'It's all been in there, waiting!'

I loved this. But I felt I had to go on and speak about the pregnancy and my shock at not being told about it. I stumbled when I came to the part about the child. My guilt, my helplessness, and I knew so little detail. Suddenly I was exposed. We sat with it together in silence.

'And you, my beloved Fran, you lost a child. It must have been awful for you. How old were you? The same as me of course. We were students, ignorant, innocent, helpless.'

'Yes, we were.' She was thoughtful.

I looked at her, she looked so young, so beautiful. I

asked, 'Have you ever thought of having another child?'

She was quiet. 'No. Perhaps this is the same for both of us. Since we're speaking openly – I imagine you never had the chance of another child with Emily because of celibacy.'

I nodded. 'And my choosing someone like Emily, choosing the role I played in the marriage, we never matured enough to become parents sadly. I have never thought of having a child, not since Frances. Our child was lost.'

'Like Agnes' child,' she said quietly. 'And mine of course. What unlived lives we share, don't we Max ....'

There was a short silence, before she continued, 'During the birth I had complications. I was told I would not be able to have children after this. I was sad of course, very sad. But I did not feel guilty like you did.' She shrugged. 'I was young and, in some way, relieved. I didn't have to think about it again. When I told lovers who were possibly getting serious, they backed away if they were hoping for a life with me and children. I found them out that way. And perhaps I've lived life as a dancer, light on my feet. I've not thought about it. She learned against me, stroking my arms.

'I'm sad for you that you felt all those passions had such a high cost rather than being part of exploration. Now I know that's where you began to learn it all...not just from me eh?' She was teasing. I held her and kissed her over and over.

'Carino... We just never know what's inside of us, do we, until we begin exploring, and exploring with others, in intimacy ...' She looked suddenly serious. 'I can really understand why you became a therapist. You can help others so well, can't you? But maybe you've left yourself until last... Si?'

I was so deeply touched.

'Thank you, thank you!' I was in tears again. And so touched by her real understanding, her acceptance and her kindness...'

We sat in silence for a while. She put her head on my shoulder speaking softly.

'Your early years. Oxford, so grand, so clever a young man with his whole life ahead full of promise... such important early years, especially coming after your parents' and sister's deaths; and what you've just told me.'

I felt tearful again and reached for more hugs. She was becoming a rather wonderful therapist herself!

'It's given you a heavy heart about matters of sex and the body. But let's rejoice now in the reality of those times where you learned so much. You've helped others come to life. And me, I've lived my life trying to create other things, images, words. Los ninos, children, they are all there in what I manifest in my work.'

We talked all night and both of us fell asleep downstairs.

Chapter 18

In the autumn of that year, the leaves on the oak and beech, which had previously glowed with their golden colours, were leaving the landscape. The bare bones of their structures rooted in the increasingly bare earth echoed the gradual descent of nature into winter. The few remaining leaves on the beech hedge seemed to shiver and shake in the wind. It was dark just after 4pm. The luminous light of spring, the glorious feasts of summer and the autumn glow were no longer so evident unless they remained in memory, unseen, to light us up inside. Eliot's words were often with me. 'Be still, and let the dark come upon you ...'

Agnes walked into her session alone and had no bundle with her. It was just a month now since our visit to Salisbury Plain. She looked bereft, lost, and deeply sad, her music and movement on hold. I waited for her to speak.

'There is no hope is there? Hope with a capital H, or hope itself. The daughter I might have had is gone. She's dead. I must face it. I must face that I never knew that I was carrying a child. She was never known by me, by anyone.' She held her head in her hands. 'But why, why didn't I know? I can't believe this. It was only after I had lost her that my dreams told me she had wanted to land with me. Only after I had lost her that she began to come alive to me.'

I was moved by her clarity. She gave a huge sigh.

'It's been important to me, very important, to make this journey with you. I've learned things about living in a body – or not living in it as is my case – that I would never have learned, so this must mean something useful ... I don't know ...'

We sat together.

'I've decided that I must, whenever it appears in my or others' lives to speak of loss, any loss and whilst I am here to share this with you. It's all – all we have spoken of over these years, its all been important. I do know this.' She smiled, touching her brow. 'But that does not bring her back, does it? I will never see her alive. And, I never really saw her dead, did I?'

Her eyes were dull and sorrowful.

'But the bottom line is, that even though my unknown,

to me, pregnancy might be linked with trauma, it's still my experience. I have to live with its reality.'

I marvelled at her understanding at the same time as being aware of her suffering. She was speaking lucidly. Her body was tight, upright, on the edge of the chair. Then her body began to sag.

'The most depressing thing is to think, to wonder: can I be trusted? I feel as if I just don't deserve to be given anything. To think that I could have had and celebrated a live child. Think of that ... what is the matter with me that I cannot accept goodness when it comes my way?'

There was pleading in her eyes. What she had just said was a really powerful realisation. And I knew myself exactly how she felt. I too had been unable to be aware of the gifts possible in living in a body, for I had shunned them out of guilt just as I was beginning to find them. A guilt that had always been there, driving me on into self-negation and shame. Much was beginning to become conscious and to be shared for both Agnes and me, especially after my recent conversations with Fran. We had both allowed ourselves to be sad together about our own lost children, children that might have been. And alongside this our unlived lives, inside and manifested outside. I focussed on Agnes.

'Have you left Hope at home?' I was immediately aware of the play on words.

'Hope,' she said, 'how stupid. Just a stupid delusion. I'm surprised you and Carole went along with it. It was all just play acting, wasn't it?'

'Was it?'

'Of course it was.'

She sounded angry under the sense of defeat. The grey scarf was back. She wrapped her cardigan further around her, as she twisted the familiar scarf round and round her hands. I leaned toward her.

'What happened on Salisbury Plain was important, Agnes. It was real in the sense that those were your experiences. They brought many things to the surface for you to consider, your courage, your ability to look into the dark, your ability to form attachments and to play and to love. Where your repression of them might have originated is something we will speak more about.'

I paused, concerned about going on too long, being too serious, too theoretical.

'But in those moments, there on the Plain, you genuinely experienced darkness and you fought back against what seemed to be dangerous demons. They are externalised symbols if you like for all the aggression you have experienced in your life. And also, the darkness you sensed so vividly in Cracow and at Birkenau. In those moments, in the place of both birth and death, you faced darkness full on and chose life. You saw the figures of darkness off and then ran and ran until you found a symbol of new life. And of hope.'

Her shoulders slumped. She got up and walked around.

'It's all so abstract though, isn't it? I just can't face the reality of it. That I allowed a child to die. Inside and outside of me.'

'What happened all happened unconsciously, Agnes. It was not a conscious act to deny your pregnancy. I imagine that if you had had a glimpse of the possibility of being pregnant you would have been pretty scared. You would most probably have banished the thought. It was not something you could face or endure.' I paused. 'Your body did this for you, concealing any awareness of pregnancy as a protection.'

'But the reality ...'

'I think that you are facing the reality right now, Agnes,' I said firmly.

We sat again in silence. Our silences felt as they had so many notes and sounds in them. The lost lives of her ancestors, her own unheard calls to her mother, the silencing of any inner dialogue, so many lost notes of potential communication.

'Your current depressed feelings and puzzlement are a natural response to the events all those years ago Agnes, as well as the more recent ones. Our visit to Salisbury Plain' she flinched at the words 'began an awakening process to the reality and presence of your child which you were unable to do after Cracow. All that and you are now facing and finding ways to bear the reality that the daughter you might now be holding in your arms or watching play is dead. It's a deep, deep sadness.'

She had indeed entered a time of depression. I was concerned for her, but I felt she needed to be inside the reality of her many losses and to be able to lament them and allow her recent experiences to become real. The bundle she brought back from the Plain had given her time, as well as the possibility of hope. I thought again about Eliot: 'wait without hope for hope would be hope for the wrong thing'. She had enjoyed her bundle of hope, it had given her time, but now was the time to experience what might arise within the non-attachment of waiting. Waiting in the unknown. That she had found hope was undeniable, but it seemed as if it must not be hope as an escape exit, but that she allowed herself time to find a different experience of hope, one that arose from finding trust and sharing her experience of darkness and loss. Hope for a more open and free flexible life for herself. Hope for peace of mind.

I also was in some new darkness. The reappearance of Emily that weekend in Suffolk felt bleak. Even though there were so many points of contact between Fran and I, it was as if the wonder, the magic and bloom, had started to lessen. I did not want this but how could I recreate it, find a way to nourish and hold onto it? Had we been just like adolescent innocents floating above reality and now we had come down to earth? Or was this simply an ordinary part of building a relationship where only time would tell what was possible or where we might be going. If so, was the magic ever real? Was I being adolescent? I just felt heavy hearted.

Emily did not come back to the cottage that next day after surprising me. I had decided it was best if Fran stay away walking Millie whilst I spoke firmly to Emily. I waited there all morning, and I tried looking for her in the village, asking people if they had seen a woman in an old grey mac walking alone. But I never found her or any information about her. I returned to London, tormented once again by my old sense of responsibility. And of course, the inevitable 'what ifs. What if she had walked into the sea like Margaret? That thought made me tremble. She knew about my sister of course, and that we were twins and close, and that I had often blamed myself for not knowing how desperate she had become when she drowned herself just near to the cottage. I was enjoying myself at Oxford; so many punishments for pleasure I was realising ... always having to pay for enjoyment, so why not now? Why not just as I was enjoying times with Fran and enjoying the work with Agnes?

I was to find out when I returned to Suffolk the following weekend that on the Monday after our encounter Fran had seen Emily walking on the beach and called to her. Emily had frozen and then run off. But Fran followed slowly with Millie and eventually caught up with her, sitting on a bench near the fishermen's huts. She was weeping. To my amazement, Fran told me they had spoken together. When I heard this relief surged through every cell in my body and a warm and unfamiliar feeling of being supported followed.

Emily of course complained about me, and my self-importance. Fran just listened, although she teased me later! Apparently, Emily's partner in Devon, Shirley, had become increasingly unwell after being diagnosed with MS. Her moods changed and at times her behaviour became challenging. Emily had simply walked out, unable to manage it anymore. I didn't know much about the basis of their relationship, but I did know that Emily was used to being the one looked after, the 'poorly one', and I doubted that she had learned many caring skills. Fran had listened to her as she let off steam and then they had walked along the beach talking for some time. Fran asked what Emily had hoped she would achieve by coming to see Max. At that she had put on her sullen face again, the face she had showed to both of us outside the cottage door.

'Gosh,' said Fran, 'to think that you tolerated that all those years.'

I protested, but Fran put her hand over my mouth and said, 'Just listen. You've got a friend here. Take it in ... I'm not judging either of you.'

It appeared that Emily thought that as I 'rescued' her once I would do so again. She said that secretly she thought I wasn't a sexual man and never dreamt that I would meet another woman. She had said, 'Well he was 'nearly a monk', to which Fran said, bravely I thought, 'But I understand that suited you, didn't it?' and Emily had looked startled and angry.

It was as if she had never considered me as a separate person from the role I played in her life. Nor did she consider that

I might not want to see her, let alone 'rescue her' again. I found it all uncomfortable. It also made me feel very sad for what felt like lost life, lost time. Emily and I, were we both waiting for something, someone to come along and change things or change us? Or were we simply unconscious? I was unaware that I might have been waiting. Perhaps I could have lived the life of a monk. My Buddhist practice was important to me, essential for how I lived my life and nourished my understanding. Meeting Fran had brought in another dimension to being present with the joy of living in a body and to be truly present with each moment with wonder and gratitude. When I had this thought, I turned to her and held her closely. 'You have woken me haven't you, darling? You've woken me up to another aspect of myself. You've made me feel respect for myself and a whole man with appetites as well as discipline and given me the courage to live fully.'

Fran had encouraged Emily to go back to Devon, contact some of the friends she had made there and see if she could stay with them whilst she tried to talk more with Shirley. Emily even gave her address to Fran, who asked her to let her know how it all worked out. Emily realised that she felt ashamed she had let Shirley down. It seemed as if the two women did love each other.

I thought about the tortured Sunday night back in London I had given myself wondering about Emily and what I would do if she rang me with threats of suicide. I would have had to go to her I was sure ... And worse still were fears she might actually take her own life. The two contrasts, between my old limited, trapped thinking and Fran's open generosity and freedom, gave me much to ponder on.

These events were transformative for me, and I took some of the energy of this joy and evidence for change into my work with Agnes. It felt as if in the often long but comfortable silences Agnes had been able to reflect more on her own history. This became the new music we moved into, a new composition of meaningful pauses and silences. We were yet to find already composed pieces that would suit the time and so we weathered on with what we already had, our years spent sitting and focussing together. She wept and grieved. One of her poems had the line: 'My body knows something before I do. In its hurt, its pain, its fear. The way it shuts down. It's only when you stop that you can hear your own grief.'

She began weaving words into what had been the wordless threads of her life, woven with her easy adaptability, ability to please and work hard in life. Part of this journey were her now regular visits to her mother. She felt that her experience of Poland, of the millions of lost lives had awakened her to something deeper and that she could find the courage to explore it more. What she said was deeply moving: 'I've had the opportunity here to be listened to and to learn to listen. I was too frightened to listen before to myself. The birds and trees did it for me!'

She looked at me directly, something she did increasingly, barefaced without the covering of the scarf. She had a great beauty and presence in those moments.

'And you have shown me kindness and respect. If I have been fortunate enough to have received these gifts, I want to share them. And my mother seems to be in need. And' she looked serious, 'it's something of a journey for me, speaking with her differently.'

It was as if she had decided to visit her mother again because, possibly a bit like me, there was more space inside her to make choices and a new freedom, she had nothing to lose.

'If it doesn't sound too grandiose, sometimes I can sense the souls of Birkenau calling to me... my great grandparents, my grandparents and so many others. All so traumatised. And I welcome this calling. Theirs were lost lives like my own child, lost hope, and if there is anything I can offer in the way of healing then I want to offer it. If there is some form of new life I can offer against all this horror then I know I must follow it.'

We allowed a warm silence. I was again moved by her awakening.

'My mother has not ever been able to hear, to hear anything of this past so tightly held within her. She hasn't been able to look at me properly, but now I am beginning to have different conversations with her...'

They fed and watched the birds together, and one day a goldfinch arrived. A first. As she watched this glorious and rare bird feeding so delicately, she quietly asked her mother to speak more about her own childhood and to ask again if she ever wondered about her ancestors in Poland. Her mother did not snap or walk out but said, 'I've always wanted to go there. Like you have. But I never had the courage. You've got more than me. I did look at the photos you showed me, and I did wonder how my parents had lived. But of course, I never knew them.'

She was near to tears, a rare event. Then rather amazingly she said, 'My mother died in childbirth as you know…I've thought about what you said…

'Perhaps I caused her death. And you also, by not knowing of your pregnancy, you also have this cross to bear.'

They had held each other's arms and sat together in this new, warm silence, the echoes of the past around them.

Chapter 19

At first my Christmas break from work felt bleak for me that year. Fran had gone back to Barcelona to spend Christmas with her elderly mother. I went alone to the cottage in Suffolk and walked my usual routes along the beach, a beach so full of memories and associations, past and present.

My one shining light, with me constantly, was Millie! Fran had entrusted her beloved dog Millie to me for most of her time away. I collected her from Fran's Suffolk neighbour who had had her for a few days, and I was to look after her for the rest of the three weeks Fran was in Spain. I'd not had responsibility for a dog before, and it was both slightly alarming but also comforting. Millie had got to know me during these months and I her. She would jump on my knee when I was listening to music or try to get up there when I was at the piano. She'd look at me with her huge brown eyes in a sort of pleading way, as if trying to communicate. Every day I wondered if she missed Fran and I am sure she did, but she seemed comfortable, coming with me on long walks and letting me tend to her. I took her to London when I returned to work for the last week of Fran's absence, and we did some of the familiar things from the times when she and Fran had stayed with me there. But clearly, like me, she preferred Suffolk, and I realised increasingly, so did I. Her enthusiasm on our return there was evident, as was mine! We would both run out of the cottage in the afternoons and early mornings and scamper on the beach whatever the tide or weather.

As I write this now, I realise how reflective and open I was starting to feel that Christmas and New Year, just over two years ago now. It felt as if many things were beginning to come together, and many understandings were deepened. For the first time I began to ponder on what I really wanted without the burden of guilt!

Those walks, in the company of a dog who right from our first meeting had brought me down to a watery earth, touched on so many past themes as I passed the familiar shores and the slowly falling sandy coastline. Memories of both death and of new life. I was struck more forcibly by what I felt was the powerful ever-present reality of change and loss. Of death, and of rebirth. Dunwich, now a small village with one main street was once a huge thriving medieval port with several thousand inhabitants. It had several churches and spaces for gatherings celebrating many different approaches to life and death. After one huge storm at sea the city's future was sealed. Over time the houses and streets gradually crumbled and fell as the sandy cliffs were eroded by the waves.

After this year of listening to Agnes and her calls to her own lost ancestors I also pondered on the echo of all the lost souls who had once lived here, in this lost city now taken by the sea. And the many places of worship also taken by the waves. The sandy cliffs were still eroding year by year. I pondered more deeply on the call of the sea and the waves and remembered a teacher I had once who said that 'suffering needed to be taken on wave only,' meaning one wave at a time, slowly. And in meditation we often speak of the in and out breath being like a wave, rising and falling.

And of course, my own individual path of history here. Always there were images and memories of Margaret. She and I walking and talking on that beach especially after the loss of our parents as we were enduring the shifts of adolescence and feeling very alone. And her last moments here when she had walked into those waves one early morning. I would look out at the horizon thinking about her and wondering, over and over but of course receiving no answers: what was she thinking then if she was thinking at all, what was she feeling? The bleak horror of that desperate final act, to destroy one's own life because of... so many unknowns... But also, for dear Margaret there had most certainly been an unbearable unhappiness, and for many years. She came up against the impossibility of continuing life, or, perhaps, she heard the call of something else?

And now, after these tumultuous years of working with Agnes I also thought of all those other lost souls who had been rounded up in great waves all over Germany and Poland, sacrificed to idealism, tortured, imprisoned, persecuted, threatened before perishing in the camps of Birkenau. Children, young people, old people, people who didn't fit it, who didn't belong because of the group into which they were born.

Margaret, she also never felt she fitted in, nor did she

want to. But the huge difference was that she had choice.

I remembered so many other walks on this beach, meaningful walks where I encountered different, often troubled thoughts. Sometimes the strides into the wind, the calls of the gulls, the wading birds, starfish, sea spray… the history of this place, sometimes those were present, my beach memories.

And of course, there was my meeting with Fran. The joy of that day when I followed Millie into the waves. Millie, here by my side each day racing in and out of the waves and looking at me earnestly hoping I would fall in again to play. Oh Fran, darling Fran. I thought of her constantly. I thought my heart would burst. A new feeling so different from all those years of constriction. The light she brought into my heart, my whole being. It was a precious jewel, a pearl that I cherished. She had changed the lens through which I had seen myself for so long. I stood and watched the waves speaking aloud to her, and to both of us, singing our favourite songs.

As the days went on it felt as if I was being invited into deeper reflections and contemplations and on several different levels. There were contemplations on these past therapeutic years with Agnes and what she and her ancestors had been through, with my being invited into material so deep, and collective. And the deep, deep sorrow left from these times. And in contrast there was the joy and life-giving energy of these few months with Fran. I decided to practice more walking meditations which meant going really slowly, step by step, feeling my feet touching the earth in all its myriad forms here on the beach. The grit and stones possibly once part of a great church; the ever-shifting sand; the salty sea water. Millie would look at me curiously then go her own way rushing ahead, chasing other dogs, diving into the sea and sniffing around quite happily. These walking meditations twice each day allowed me to reflect more deeply on many things and events. They had an energy of their own. I noticed that I often touched my chest, sometimes my heart area as Carole and Philip had done before, when I did not fully understand why. But they did. One day I stopped and kneeled on the wet stony sand. Tears ran down my cheeks. In Bearing Witness Bernie Glassman had written about the discovery of love that was always involved in bearing the impact of the past; and that there were many ways to express a broken heart. This image is often used so generally it can be dismissed as fanciful, just an idea without any thought or pondering. But the heart can be touched and broken emotionally in so many ways, individually or collectively without understanding about the possible myriad meanings. And those ultimate questions: 'what does your heart mean to you?' And 'if your heart could speak what would he or she say?'

All this, my search for true in depth meaning, entered my awareness. My Buddhist practice had taught me much about the heart and words and images were present. Renowned teacher Pema Chodron says that we can open our hearts to the pain of what has been unworked through. In doing so we join others and are not alone. Therapy can also offer that experience. We dare to open our hearts and feel the opening in the shared safe presence of an understanding other. Waking up means that the door to our heart can be left open, the door of compassion. I believed that in sharing and bearing past patterns, both dark and light, we find choice. A choice to accept, make peace and heal; or, to continually blame, lament, engage with rage and anger. I remembered one of the young monks in Switzerland saying, 'you don't find wholeness until you're ready to be broken.' I have understood this as being broken open from learned survival rigid patterns. It's not a breaking created by violence, but an opening and subsequent healing that emerges from choice. Potentially it's available to everyone but it is a definite choice. How we recognise that choice and to choose it is another journey. I smiled when I had this thought. 'To choose what has already chosen us.' Ah yes, it was there all along. But before this there is quite a lot of waiting and old learned patterns and beliefs constantly pulling!

My walks were so eventful internally, it was like a fruitful journey gathering past wisdoms and, for the first time bringing in my most recent experiences of joy and of attempting to let go of the old.

One early morning as the sun was just rising, I realised that I wanted to think more about Fran and me, and about our potential future. I let this thought hover in my mind and heart so that it could find its true and full expression.

The very next morning, walking early with Millie who

never minded what time it was, I looked into the first rays of the winter sun and knew for certain that I wanted to find a way for my relationship with Fran to continue, in a structure that suited both our need for togetherness and intimacy and also spaciousness and aloneness. I felt that we both wanted commitment but commitment which included huge freedoms. A pair of what I thought were terns flew up from one of the waves. It was too early for their elaborate courtship dance above, but this sight seemed highly symbolic in relation to my ponderings about Fran. Such freedom, to dance and sing, to be alone and separate as well as together! I did not need to save her as I felt compelled to save Emily, and as last year seeing her again and standing up to her had taught me. I could see so clearly how claustrophobic and suffocating it had been for both of us. Wow. I sank onto the wet sand and Millie danced around me licking my salty face and ears.

More ponderings: perhaps Fran and I could share the cottage together in Suffolk and she could have more space to write when I went to work in London. I imagined that she would have more commissions. Perhaps I could even come with her on assignments. I did not know how long I would go on seeing patients, but I could remain open to different possibilities. And travelling with Fran would be one of them.

I returned to London and to work in January, resuming sessions with Agnes. She was still depressed, but she was also reflective. I felt that it was a potentially useful time for her; to feel that she did not have to rush about and fill every moment for fear of emptiness. We could view this time of depression and low energy as an opportunity to see what might arise afresh, what might be able to come forward within the spaces invited. She might begin to allow herself to feel whatever might be wanting to arise without judgement. There were many long silences and I felt for her, hoping that she might trust herself enough to allow spaciousness and compassion. She was clearly grieving, and on so many different levels. I could name this with her, and she nodded at times, looking interested. We could speak about the different forms of grief and its passage, and how important it was. It was still hard for her to speak of the child she had named as Hope, that all seemed somewhere else, a fantasy she declared frequently. She expressed again her shame and fear that there had been something seriously wrong with her. The concept of her carrying a child inside her body was still alien and at times she would even consider herself mad or not normal. These were her harshest thoughts. There were times when she allowed herself to feel a really deep sadness for never knowing her child, never having the pleasure of being aware of her inside or outside. She could see it was a definite loss and at times she wept for this.

She had maintained contact with her mother and, although still awkward and at times painful for both of them, it felt as if something new was trying to develop. Or perhaps to be born, I thought to myself. For births and deaths featured strongly in her mother's history, births and deaths whose impact she had had to repress deeply in order to manage. I felt very moved that Agnes was finding a way to reach out to her mother despite her verbal barbs, and she was doing this in a creative determined way, not masochistic. It started with the bird feeder, something small but something which celebrated new life and it seemed to be their initial shared point of contact.

There was also of course Agnes' love of music and teaching young people the piano and singing. She and I shared less music together and I respected this as it felt as if Agnes needed the silence, the blank canvas within which to receive thoughts, feelings, ideas. Perhaps allowing the new to arise, to be born in the wordless spaces. And I was also aware: can I let this new light be born within me? We did share much of this spaciousness. When there was less darkness in the energy of the room, I could sense her expanding, breathing in and out in greater relaxation, and allowing the unknown to make her or himself known. When I said, 'I can feel your breath expanding, you seem to be able to allow the outbreath to be longer.' She smiled. 'Is there less darkness when you can enjoy simple breathing in and out?' She would nod and we would sit together enjoying simple breathing, following the breath down on the outbreath. I did feel the deep nonverbal connection we had manifested together, and I hoped that I was bringing some of the joy and resolution I was finding in my own life into the energy between us. Certainly, I hoped we might be sharing the potential for new life for both of us and moving on from trying to strive or save. Small but important steps. I remembered my own analyst's comment: 'There's nothing wrong with crumbs...'

I remembered the joy that had been awakened inside me on the beach during the Christmas break and to carry it with me everywhere. I liked to think that the warmth of our encounter and now deepening relationship was moving through me and could be brought into the sessions with Agnes. And Eliot's poem of course was ever present. The waiting, in the dark without hope for hope would be hope for the wrong thing. And I wondered over and over, what did I hope for Agnes, did I have a hope or even a goal? Not that I liked this word in relation to therapy. We travel with the unknown, in each participant and often the fruits of therapy are not revealed until years later.

Fran was back to Millie's delight, and we spent long weekends together in Suffolk, continuing to enjoy each moment and gently, tenderly discussing the future.

Just before the Easter break Agnes told me that she and Carole had been discussing going to Salisbury Plain for Easter. The image of that place and our October visit entered the room. She smiled when she said, 'well doctor, it's death and rebirth time isn't it? We will go to St Matthew Passion on the Sunday, there is a concert in Salisbury, and we've booked in. We will do everything consciously this time. Hope did pave the way and I'm glad I went with you just before I allowed the dark to take over.'

I was delighted and happy with their plans, it felt good they would be sharing this together. I was at the same time concerned about the unexpected and what they might experience this time. But this was their decision, they had both been through so much and learned a lot from it. I told myself I needed to question my old pattern of caution and fear over any new adventure!

Fran and I went to Scotland over Easter. She worked some of the time and we walked in the early mornings and late afternoons along the coast. We also managed a couple of days on the island of Islay where the barnacle geese winter in great flocks and thrilled us with their noisy gathering. We watched peregrine falcons and fulmars swooping above. Millie loved all of it of course and I felt as if we were beginning to be a little family together.

When I saw Agnes again, I sensed that we were now moving into the final months of our work together. She took a couple of months to name this, but we agreed that it could be time and named the date of our last session as the end of July. Her visit to Salisbury Plain with Carole had been extremely therapeutic. They had visited the hospital where Agnes had been taken and asked to see the place where her child's ashes had been scattered. Five years on she knelt in the place and wept, her tears moistening the ground. She lamented and cried, Carole standing by giving her time and space. She went to visit the couple who had found her curled up on the Plain to give thanks to them for getting help. She told me that they were amazed by her story and her complex journey and touched that she had been to visit them.

Then she and Carole went to Salisbury Plain with flowers and incense. They walked round the great stones and made an offering near to the place where Agnes' body seemed to direct them. Agnes was amazed to experience this natural process of her body and was very moved. As was I, so happy.

'Carole and I sat there, on the ground, and sang songs about a child who was destined not to live in this time and space as a human child but who was destined to bring all kinds of other life into mine. And my loved ones.'

She sang one of the songs to me and it was really beautiful, haunting and reverent. She and Carole had created several more songs for their time on the Plain. They were all deeply moving, and the last one Agnes alone sang to me was connected to her new awareness of the child who wanted to land with her.

'I am slowly finding the land of
Hope.
So small, she wanted to land with me.
I have been looking for her land.
Now I have found it.
It is here, and now.
She is here.
Hope brings light.

Hope is alive within me.
Hope has come alive.
Her light shines on the lost souls in the past.
Hope is for those who have been denied life.'

Chapter 20

Two years on from ending the therapy with Agnes, Fran and I continue to enjoy our relationship which grows and grows. Every day I marvel at it. I spend more time in Suffolk and only work two days a week in London. I rent my London flat to someone who works in London three days a week. It is a good arrangement and brings in an income. Fran stays at my cottage in Suffolk when she is in the UK and is still writing and illustrating more books. We created a study for her in one of the upstairs bedrooms with views across the heath. Her book about the birds of three of the English coasts is published in Spain and the UK and doing well. We have travelled together exploring more of Europe and the Scottish islands which she loves. I am still trying to learn Spanish properly and can get by reasonably well, although often I notice an amused smile on Fran's face. I had to practice hard on my new Spanish vocabulary and pronunciation before I met her mother, and this seemed to go OK. Her mother smiled at me, nodding, and beamed at Fran.

'Oh, so charming you are, dottore Maxwell' Fran sang to me afterwards. And I fell in love with Barcelona and wondered whether one day we might be able to buy a place there together. How wonderful that would be. I might even begin writing myself.

There is deep joy, but of course, it is not without stabs of doubt and fear that still find their way in every now and then. Not surprising after sixty something years! Was I really allowed all of this? All this happiness? In brave moments I nod to it, 'ah my friend guilt, I see you are still there in the corners of the past, haunting me... to keep me from... ?' From what, from my taking it all for granted? I made sure I did not. I treasured every day. Guilt, as ever, especially magical guilt, is a powerful energy and I knew that I must guard and treasure my newfound joy, every minute of it and relish the newfound life.

I hoped very much that Agnes had been able to do the same. To hold onto her newfound happiness and new life.

It was time for Agnes visit. I received cards from her at both Christmases since she completed therapy, words of greeting and gratitude, but no particular news about her activities. So I am interested in what she might be bringing and what is new in her life.

She confirmed our meeting recently and indicated that she would be coming with Carole and that they had something to show me.

I had been looking forward to seeing them and curious. I was also curious about my sense of anticipation about what they might be bringing. I wondered if I was fearing some other catastrophe. The 'yes... but... 'attitude. But when I opened the door and saw their radiant faces and smiles, I relaxed, hoping that what they were bringing was connected to the sense of new life and light that Agnes had discovered and which, possibly, they had nurtured together. They smiled back and Agnes stepped forward to give me a huge hug.

'You are allowed' she said laughing, 'and I am allowed.'

Carole nodded, also smiling broadly. They stepped into my consulting room.

'So,' said Agnes, 'you are only here two days a week now? I hope life is good for you.'

'It is indeed' I smiled, inviting them to sit.

There was a warm comfortable silence as I noticed each of them taking in the room, still exactly the same as when they left with its familiar things, the piano they had both played many times, several sea paintings, views through the window of the magnolia still fully green, the Tibetan bell.

Agnes sighed and murmured, 'All that I experienced here in this room. All that I learned. I have said this before, but I learned so much here, with you.' She looked serious and nodded. 'I did find life here and hope of course, with a small and a capital H.'

'And me too,' Carole added.

They looked at each other. Carole nodded to Agnes, and she looked at me directly.

'We wanted to come together to see you and to let you know of our continuation. We have continued to create music, individually and together. Music that celebrates the themes of healing and rebirth that came alive in this room with you Dr Max. Hope has landed safely and is alive through us.'

She looked towards Carole and reached out her hand to

hers.

'We live together now, and we can say more about that and how we've recently moved into a marvellous place - an old spacious shop we've been doing up, thanks to being sponsored by someone who attends our concerts regularly. We still have our day jobs but, in the evenings, and at weekends we've been creating musical happenings in different forms. Anna joined us at the beginning and now her friend Mary, and partner Alec, also musicians, who specialise in traditional music have joined in this venture. We wanted to create music that would include both sorrow and joy.' They looked at each other. 'We've both seen how dark human beings and life can be. We've both known sadness, trauma, externally and internally. And beginning here in this room we've found ways to be with it so that if possible, some form of new life may arise where once there was devastation, even death.'

We sat together, all moved by these words.

'We began running regular composition classes, inviting people to come and create their own music. These, and our musical evenings became popular in our part of east London. From some of the proceeds of these concerts we have also created special programmes for children from refugee communities to whom we are able to teach an instrument. And to listen to the sounds of their own music. We have several old instruments now that we've collected or have been donated, and we invite the children to choose one and have a go with it. They are shy at first, but they come with a parent or minder who keeps an eye on them, and Carole and I play together to encourage them. The children take to it all so well and comfortably. We've had concerts with them, and they've proved very popular indeed.'

There was a joyous pause. We all smiled.

'Music is in all our souls,' I said. I felt so very happy.

'As Agnes said earlier, we live together now,' Carole said her eyes shining. 'We have this rather wonderful place that we've been able to rent and would like to be able to buy one day. It's an old shop that had been empty for years. The big downstairs room has been great for holding musical happenings. Last year we entered a BBC competition for amateur musicians with one of our compositions and we came second so we've been on the radio and are about to go on television. We wanted to play you some of our creations today and to celebrate with you. Listening in a particular heartfelt way to music led the way for all of us here to open to something else. The gathering of the souls of suffering has become our mission. We are thinking of creating a charity and we wanted you to be involved, to be our chairman or patron. That is, if you are happy to do this?'

I was really choked. They had such energy, such obvious happiness. My heart was full indeed. I managed to say that I would be honoured.

Then Agnes went to the piano and began to play, and Carole took out a small pipe and began to join her. There was a chorus in which they both sang together. We all were warmed and moved by the sound created whilst outside the glorious maple and the magnolia glowed in full leaf.

Waterlilies. Opening and closing.
Each day different.
Ripples on the surface of a pond.
Water boatman. Newt.
Heron rising slowly over water.
Tawny owl calls at dusk.
The taste of wild blackberries
Smell of wet earth after rain.

It's never too late to join
All animate life
And look into the eye of another with genuine kindness.

Waterlilies
Ripples on a pond
The flight of the goldfinch

This moment
This only
All that there is.